Ben Mulligan is a cop from the Northern Territory town of Katherine, with more than his share of problems.

When he heads down to Camp Leichhardt, a Grey Nomad camp on the Roper River, to fish and get away from the stresses of life, he finds that all is not what it seems. Ben uncovers a criminal conspiracy that will destroy lives and wreak havoc on local communities.

With the beautiful Malea as his ally, he has to face his past head on, and tackle a cartel intent on making money at any cost. Yet, in doing so, he risks everything, even his own future.

Also by Greg Barron:

 HarperCollins*Publishers* Australia

Rotten Gods
Savage Tide
Lethal Sky
Voodoo Dawn (short fiction)

STORIES OF
OZ

The Hammer of Ramenskoye (short fiction)
Camp Leichhardt
Galloping Jones and Other True Stories from Australia's
History
Whistler's Bones
Red Jack and the Ragged Thirteen
Outlaw: The Story of Joe Flick
The Time of Thunder
The Last Days of Dom Sebastian
The Pedestrian
Wild Dog River

For younger readers:

High Country Caper
Gulf Country Gambit

Camp Leichhardt

Greg Barron

First published 2017
This edition 2025
by **Stories of Oz** Publishing
PO Box K57
Haymarket NSW 1240

ABN: 0920230558
facebook.com/storiesofoz
ozbookstore.com

© 2025 Greg Barron
ISBN: 9780648062707
Proof reading: Tegan Hall
Cover image photography: Zoe Knight
Typeset in 12/16 point Bembo
Printed and bound in Australia by IngramSpark

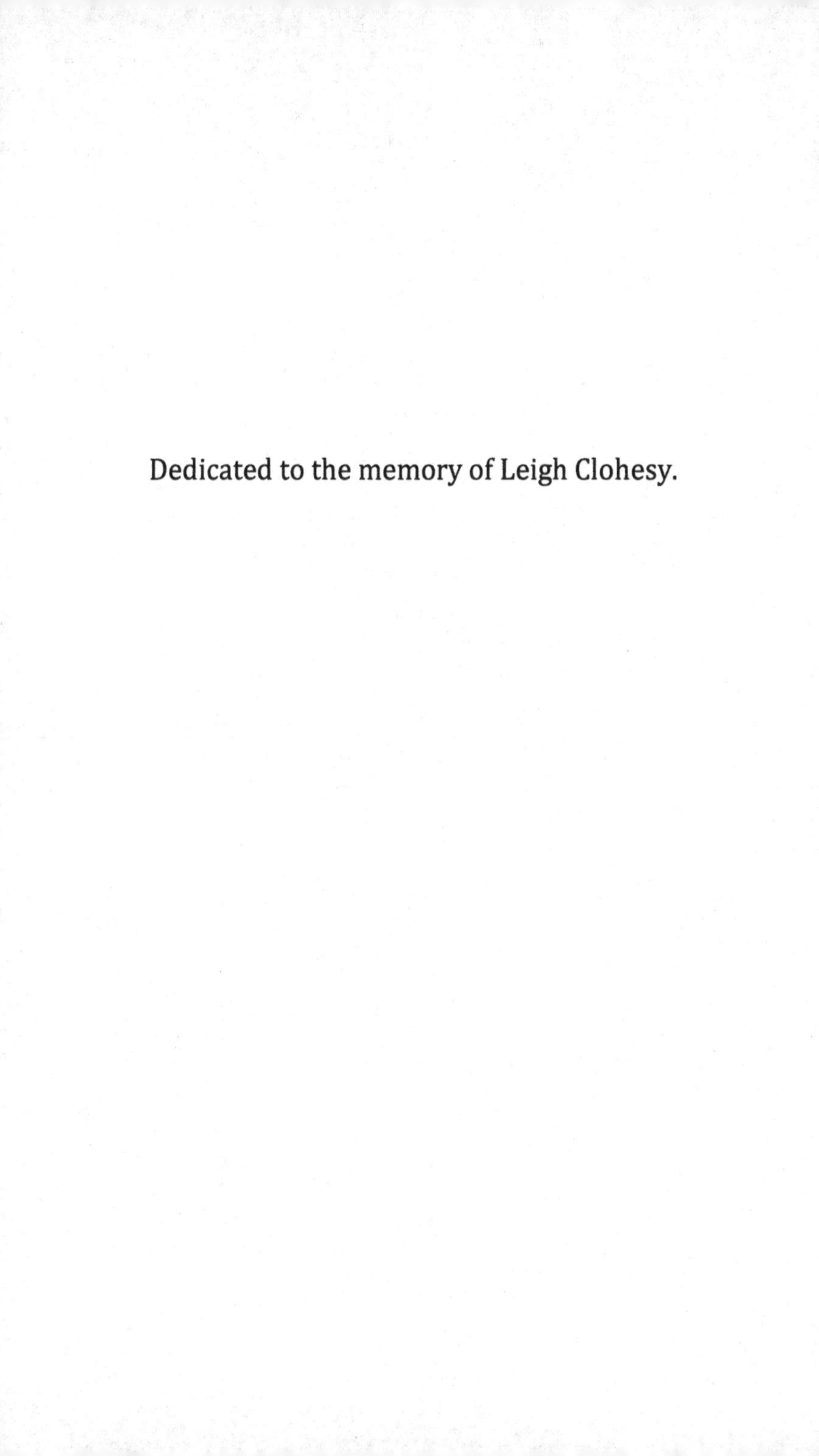

Dedicated to the memory of Leigh Clohesy.

Chapter One

WITH A STRONG sense of homecoming I took in the dusty sign and turned onto the narrow, rutted trail. I hadn't been down to Camp Leichhardt for five years, but I treasured the memory like a warm stone in my heart. This was the place I remembered when things were tough back in Katherine.

The track in from the highway showed the wear and tear of regular traffic, bulldust pits that had the 70-Series LandCruiser slipping and sliding, spewing up a reddish cloud from the Toyo M55s. The suspension rocked and squeaked, gears crunched, and the sun glared through a grit-streaked windscreen onto my hands and forearms.

The trees were bigger near the river – woollybutt and ghost gum – scattered pandanus throwing off limp brown fronds. Stands of casuarina fringed the sand gullies, with nagura burr and hiptus in the clearings.

Over the second jump-up I had my first view of the Roper. Green and majestic in the channel she had, over millions of years, carved into the plain, fringed with spiral pandanus and mangroves with their shiny waxed leaves. The moist air met me through the open window, and I sniffed at it like a drunk.

The track followed the first gully behind the river for a sandy kilometre or two, and I throttled back, just in time to miss a half-grown agile wallaby that burst out in front of me.

Finally, over one final hump, and there was Camp Leichhardt. Last time I was here it consisted of an old timer in a tin shanty, a few tents and five or six vans. Now the area back from the river bristled with caravans, three or four dozen, each with its own territory of around a thousand square metres. I stopped the car, engine idling, and studied the scene.

Most of the vans had a LandCruiser, Ranger, Land Rover or Patrol parked alongside, with the odd RAM or F-series Ford. At least half had a tinny, complete with a shiny new outboard on the transom. Aussie flags waved from poles beside satellite dishes and UHF aerials. Smoke rose from fires here and there, but many of the sites were empty of people and boats. I had to assume that they were out on the river.

I would have preferred to find myself a secluded spot away from the Grey Nomads, but my Stessl tinnie – on the trailer behind the Toyota – was no lightweight. Bank launching was possible but difficult. Camp Leichhardt had the best ramp for a hundred kilometres in either direction, apart from Roper Bar with its store and unofficial campsites beside the crossing – but it was too close to the road – saw too much passing traffic. No place to unwind.

The decision made, I eased my foot off the brake and onto the accelerator. A few oldies wouldn't be too bad. They would certainly mind their own business. As I drove in I got a closer look at the caravans. Mostly new – Coromal, Jayco, Galaxy, Paramount, Scenic, Viscount, Windsor, Bushtracker – even a motor home or two. Some had place-name bumper stickers plastered on the rear of the van. Towns conquered like a Spitfire pilot conquered Messerschmitts. Rockhampton: Beef Capital. Winton: Dinosaur Territory. I GOT STUNG AT AUGATHELLA.

Every town and city has its claim to fame, and the Nomads, armed with their gazetteers, iPads, and paperback guides, are insatiably curious about what makes these places tick.

Here at Camp Leichhardt most were set up for a long stay. Annexes with shade cloth floors, generators in sandbagged pits; even washing machines. People sweeping, cooking, and watching TV. One Nomad sat on his arse beside his boat trailer, repacking the bearings, two of his mates watching on, beer stubbies in hand. I could smell the grease through the open window. They looked up and waved as I passed.

After a full circuit, picking out a couple of possible camping sites, an old bloke with knobby legs and shorts hitched too high on his waist limped from a shitty old van, waving in an effort to pull me over. I braked, idling while two arthritic hands, with swollen knuckles and spots on the skin that looked like mould, gripped the door sill. He was a curious looking old fellow: all bone, face so gaunt you could see the outline of his skull. There was a scar across his forehead and one of his eyes was bung.

'How're things?' I asked.

'Good mate, good. But you was drivin' a bit fast there mate. Dust. We gotta keep the dust down – do you mind slowin' up a bit?'

'Sorry about that.' I was surprised. It seemed to me that I had crawled the whole way.

'Where are you plannin' to camp?' he asked.

I pointed to the furthest point away from most of the vans. 'Probably down there close to the river. I won't get in the way.'

He paused for a bit, staring in the direction I'd indicated, then, 'You stayin' long?'

'A week, maybe longer. Is that alright with you?' A touch of humour crept into my voice. This was public land, yet he was carrying on as if he were about to charge me a fee.

'Yeah, yeah, 'course it is.' He raised one hand off the sill and we shook. 'Me name's Davis. I'm the unofficial mayor here. We've got a bit of a committee, make decisions and all that.'

'Good to meet you, Davis. I'm Ben Mulligan.'

'On holidays?'

'Yeah. From Katherine. I'm in the police force up there.' I don't know why I told him. Maybe just to get a reaction.

The good eye flew open. 'Cop, eh?'

'Yeah, but I'm on holidays. I'm not gonna start searching people's vans or anything. All I want is a quiet spot and a fair go at the ramp.'

'Yeah, 'course, 'course. We all come from somewhere – all got other lives. Look at me – from Ballarat, down in Victoria – seven months there, five months here. Used to be a real estate agent so I still pick up a bit of work when I go back down south.' He tapped the roof of the 'Cruiser. 'You need anything, just ask me.' He pointed towards two tandem trailers, a pile of drums and a clapped-out shipping container. 'We ship fuel down from Katherine, and beer. Communal kinda thing. We've even got mobile phone coverage. Telstra put a relocatable tower in for us, see?'

I was impressed. We shook again, and I eased into first gear. Nice and slow.

I set up camp two hundred metres from the nearest of the Nomads, about the same distance from the riverbank, with a stand of casuarinas for shade. I love the way they whistle in the afternoon breeze – and they don't lose limbs like eucalypts. My tent was for storage rather than sleeping, a swag rolled out beside the fire is comfortable enough.

My old man, a surveyor working out of Darwin for thirty years, taught me the finer points of camp craft. Any idiot can make himself uncomfortable in the bush, and others so load themselves down with luxuries that they spend most of their time unpacking and repacking. The secret is simplicity, quality gear, and common sense. Within an hour I had the billy on, camp table up, and everything unpacked that needed to be unpacked.

I sat on a folding chair beside the fire, tackle box open, tying a collar and capstan knot on one of my favourite barra lures, a scarred Reidys B52 lure that might have been fifteen years old. I'd snagged it up a hundred times and each time managed to dislodge it with an oar, or even stripped off and braved the crocs to get it back.

After a quick cuppa I unstrapped the Stessl, charged the carby up with the rubber bulb and drove slowly towards the ramp, mindful of old Davis and his warning about dust. The ramp here was a good one, as bush ramps go, but narrow – needed a bit of care to back down straight. The trailer helped. I had taken the time to set her up right, with a full set of Teflon skids and fifteen-inch wheels equipped with Toyota bearings.

Pandanus fronds brushed the ally sides as I backed her down the ramp, trying to avoid the worst of the muddy ruts, submerging the trailer to just below the hubs in the river water. Leaving the engine running, I stepped out of the door, slipped the hook out of the bow eye and pushed off, taking a firm grip on the rope as I did so, leading her away and making fast to a mangrove trunk. It was high tide, and I kept a look out for crocs as I did so. A cranky, lazy old bastard usually hangs around these bush ramps, living on fish frames. It wouldn't pay to be careless.

Having secured the boat, I slipped back into the Toyota and climbed the ramp, the combination of torque and tread making short work of the muddy ruts. At the top I parked in the shade, leaving both front windows open, then walked past the fish cleaning tables towards the ramp.

I was halfway down when I heard an engine, and stopped to listen. Whoever it was appeared to be in a hurry, defying, it seemed, the local rules about speed and dust. A battered red GQ Patrol pulled up at the top of the ramp. Two men got out, both big blokes, mid-thirties or so, wearing blue singlets, shorts and thongs. One was heavier in the gut than the other, a brown beer bottle in a neoprene stubby holder gripped tight in one fist.

They seemed to be approaching me, so I stood my ground, letting them come within a few paces before they stopped. I realised that they had to be brothers. The resemblance was strong. Dark hair, jowls, noses too small for the face. The drinker took a swig and tilted his chin high.

'G'day.'

'Yeah, g'day.' I stuck out a hand. 'Ben Mulligan.'

The two shared a glance, then, as if by agreement, ignored the hand. Feeling like an idiot with my paw in mid-air I took it back, and made as if to take a step.

'Wait a minute, where are you going?' The drinker again. He was an ugly fucker, with wispy hair on his chin, and slitty little eyes.

'Fishing.'

'Hey, you're a cop, right?'

'Yeah, so what?' News obviously travelled fast.

'Well, so, we wanna know what the fuck you're doing here. We come here to get away from rules and regulations and all that shit.' He looked at his brother.

'Yeah.' The single word was his only contribution at that point.

'What's your names?' I asked.

'Terry Yates, and this is Wallaby.'

I studied them both. 'Thanks, I'll look you both

up when I get back to work.'

'Smart arse.' Wallaby was speaking now. This one had more of a double chin than jowls. 'There's three hundred miles of river for you to camp on. Why don't you find somewhere else?'

'I want to camp here.'

'Yeah, but we don't want you.'

My mood went from fragile to something else. I had travelled here to relax. So far it wasn't working. I had Terry and Wallaby Yates pegged – petty criminals – probably done time. Hated cops.

Terry came out with, 'Things can happen out here. Lotsa things.'

'Are you threatening me?'

The bloke had the biggest smile on his face, as if admiring his own cleverness. He shrugged, as if to say, maybe I am and maybe I'm not.

As far as I could see there was no point continuing the conversation. I turned and walked away. Reaching the Stessl, I untied the rope and spun her around so I could start the motor before climbing aboard. When I looked back, they were still watching me from the top of the bank.

'Go fuck yourselves,' I said under my breath as I pulled the starter cord. The outboard running sweetly now, I climbed aboard and motored out into the tide.

Chapter Two

THE ROPER has a special beauty few other rivers can match. Fed by underground springs seeping hundreds of kilometres from the Barkly Tableland, her waters are the deepest, clearest shade of green, bursting with life. Man, I love it. Something in my soul connects with it, like an appliance plugged in to just the right current.

This is a river that resonates with culture and history. The Nile of Australia's north, where for forty thousand years the traditional owners have lived, fished and traded. Where Makassars sailed upriver in their wooden praus, holds filled with dried trepang and trade goods. Of course, the activities of humans along her banks are just window dressing. The Roper's soul is her own.

Like all good fishermen I have a better than average understanding of the ecosystem in which I hunt. Here in the Roper the food web begins with a fine green and red algae that coats rocks and hangs in slimy strings in shallows and lagoons, fringing the aquatic ferns, lilies, hydrilla and ribbonwort. Zooplankton, minute creatures that under our high school microscopes looked like dragons and snakes, feed on the algae, and are eaten in turn by aquatic insects – mayflies, beetles, midges and boatmen.

All this activity attracts small fish – glassfish, bony bream and the grunters. Crustaceans also – cherabin with their long spindly claws, atyid shrimp and fiddler crabs. After that, we get to the big predators. Whiskered, fork-tail catfish. Barra. Salt and freshwater crocs. Herons. Bitterns. Pelicans. They all have their part to play in this always-changing, magical channel: so much more than just a river, winding down through a landscape that beats to a rhythm all its own.

As I gripped the tiller and throttled away upstream, I felt my stress levels fading, deliberately not wasting time thinking about the Yates brothers. Being a cop I had long ago become used to institutionalised hatred and I had locked away enough men like them not to take their attitude personally.

By the time I rounded the second bend, past a rock bar studded with herons on the northern bank, I had relaxed again, dropping the revs and watching the sounder to avoid accidents with the prop. Two and a half metres depth, three metres, four metres – I accelerated again and reached a narrow channel, sunken trees on either side, almost six metres deep in places, but averaging four. I throttled back to trolling speed, tucked the tiller under my elbow and readied the first of two rods.

In this kind of country, I like to troll two lures. One a deep diver, the other in mid water, cutting the motor to cast to the best of the structure. I rigged the diver on a Shimano Curado/T-curve combination and the other on an old Ambassadeur reel matched to a Loomis rod. With the rod butts settled into the holders on each side and the tips twitching away with the pulse of the lures, I settled down to the business of trolling as close to structure as possible without snagging up, often lifting a rod out of the holder and guiding it around a calcified trunk that rose out of the depths.

The other hazards were low, overhanging branches, capable of snapping a rod clean in half. I used an oar to fend these off, and twice I snagged up at depth. I'd invested in a clever little sliding device on Venetian blind cord to drag the lure up from the depths, and it worked a treat.

I saw the first of several crocs on that trolling run down the northern bank, a medium sized reptile of about two and half metres length, his head and back visible just out from the bank up ahead, diving when he heard the outboard, disappearing below the surface, leaving a bow wave where he had been.

I caught one fork-tail catfish, a good-sized specimen with a mouth you could put your fist into and three jagged spines standing erect like little chainsaws. I used pliers to remove the lure and let him swim away. Catfish are tasty, if a little oily, but I wanted a barra, and if I couldn't get a barra there was plenty of steak in the Engel fridge back at camp.

Luck, it seemed, was not on my side, and after an hour I abandoned the trolling and took advantage of the beginning of the ebb tide to drift along the deeper bank, casting into every scrap of structure – drowned trees, eddies, rock bars – but the best I could do was a solid bump on a deep diver. I hammered the spot a dozen more times, drawing a blank.

Remembering a creek inlet a few kilometres downstream I motored off to find it, working eddies in the main channel. I caught just one more catfish, hardly any bigger than the lure he snaffled.

Disappointed, sunset drawing close, I planed back to the ramp, where another boat had just come in, a late-model Quintrex Hornet. Two older blokes were busy winching her onto the trailer, then towing her up a few metres with the 4x4 before twisting out the bungs. By that stage I had tilted and cut the motor, slipped over the side, and was just tying up when one of the old blokes turned to me. He was a shortish man, sixty odd years – gingery, with big hands and thick parboiled arms covered in white hair.

'You must be new here,' he said. 'Haven't seen you around.'

'Yeah, just got in today.' I realised then that the other fisherman, around the far side of the boat, was not a man, but a woman.

'You do any good?'

'Nah. You?'

He raised a rust-coloured eyebrow. 'Have a look in the esky.'

I leaned over the Hornet's gunwale and lifted the lid on a blue poly fish bin. Inside were two bright silver saltwater barra floating in icy water. The biggest would have gone five or six kilos, the other about half that weight.

'Well done,' I said, subdued. Nothing hurts a fisherman more than being upstaged at the ramp. 'Where did you get them?'

'Ah, can't give away any secrets, can we?' He held out his hand. 'My name's Bill Fowler. Just about everyone calls me Chook.'

'Nice to meet you, Chook.'

'An' this is my other half, Shirley.'

Shirley shook hands like a man, and I liked her straight off. Quiet and pleasant looking, fleshy in the face and body but not excessively so. She wore one of those shapeless, massive t-shirts that hang down over everything.

'Don't go swimming here,' Chook warned me, 'not even a quick dip. There's a big salty hangs around. Crook temper. Be careful how far you go in when you launch.'

'Yeah, I figured there'd be one around.'

There was silence for a bit while I waited for them to get organised and clear the ramp.

'Maybe,' Chook said when they were done, 'you could come around to the van for tea. We'll throw a couple of fillets on.'

I hesitated. My preference would have been to spend my first night alone, but something told me that having an ally might be a good thing. 'Thanks, I'd like that. Which one's your van?'

'Twenty-foot Regal, older one, with a yellow stripe. You'll recognise the boat.'

'No worries. When?'

'About an hour. Is that alright?'

'Yeah, great.' I watched Chook and Shirley tow the Quintrex up the bank, then walked up and got the Toyota. My faith in human nature was somewhat restored. There were good people everywhere, and in most places they far outweighed the others.

This feeling, however, was temporary. Ten minutes later, when I parked the Stessl alongside my camp site, I found a collapsed tent, and the bungs out of all three twenty-litre plastic water cans that I had stacked in the shade under the casuarinas.

I had little doubt that the Yates boys had paid me a visit. The time on the river, however, had done me so much good that I didn't bother getting angry. I hammered the pegs back in, lifted the poles and cleaned up the boat. I had a fifty-litre water tank in the 'Cruiser. Things would be tight, but I'd manage.

Chapter Three

AS LUCK WOULD HAVE IT, Chook was my closest neighbour, just across the track from my camp, with a pleasant view down towards the river. He dug into a gas fridge, standing on milk crates in the annexe, bringing out two VB stubbies. He passed one into my hand before I had a chance to say anything. I looked down at the bottle and passed it back.

'Sorry, Chook, but I don't drink.'

The man gave me a look as if I was a lunatic. 'No shit?'

I shook my head. 'Gave it away two or three years ago. Never got around to taking it up again.' I reached into the insulated lunch bag near my foot and pulled out a bottle of ginger beer. The Queensland town of Bundaberg is famous for more than just rum. 'I brought my own.'

Chook had been looking increasingly perturbed, but then he smiled, as if he understood. 'You religious or something?'

'Nah, just got sick of hangovers.' The truth was I had started to rely on the stuff to forget, and it really does work – just charge yourself up and you lose that finer part of you that feels things. Blunts you down. Trouble is that getting smashed every night is a prick of a way to live. You start to lose things you don't want to lose.

Chook said, 'I was just talking to Davis. He tells me you're a cop.'

I smiled, thinking that the poor bloke must be regretting asking me over for tea – a cop and a teetotaller. 'It's not a disease, you know.'

'Course not. My second son, Brian, is a cop too, down in the Mallee, Victoria. Town called Horsham. Know it?'

I had only a vague knowledge of Southern geography. 'Heard of it. Near Bendigo?'

'Close. Brian's a Leading Constable. Got an award last year, for bravery. There was a siege, see, and he went in and disarmed the bloke, rescued two kids and a woman.' Chook's eyes misted over. Pride. A bloke's love for his son. I liked him a little more.

'Sounds like you're part of the family,' I said. 'But not everyone here thinks the same as you.'

'No? You had some trouble?'

'Only two brothers by the name of Yates. Basically told me they didn't want me camping here.'

'Pair of arseholes – troublemakers.'

I related how they had pulled my tent down and opened the bungs on my water casks.

'Tell Davis, he's supposed to deal with that kind of thing.'

'Yeah, maybe.' I don't know what I thought, exactly, back then. Maybe that if I ignored them they'd leave me alone.

'Just be careful – they're bad news and capable of anything. In fact,' he lowered his voice, 'there's something strange going on in this place.'

'What like?'

'Dunno. Can't quite put my finger on it. Lots of little things that don't add up. The Yates brothers are just part of it.'

Shirley came down the steps of the van with a pair of skinned and boned barra fillets on a tray. 'Put these on, will you, Chook darlin'. The veggies won't be long.'

'No problem, love.' Chook went up to take the tray, then paused, addressing his wife, nodding his head back at me. 'Our mate here's a bundle of surprises. He's a cop, and he don't drink.'

Shirley cocked her head and looked at me strangely. 'Really?'

Chook found it hard to cope with me not wanting a beer. Every time he went to the fridge for a stubby, which was often, he stopped at the last moment, hitched up his draw-string trousers and stared at me. 'Now, you just tell me if you change your mind. Plenty here.'

'I'll let you know.'

'You don't mind me, er, imbibin' in front of you?'

'Of course not. If I wanted a drink I would, but I don't.'

'Yeah, yeah, I just don't wanna seem rude.'

'You're not. Honestly.'

Shirley took me under her wing, giving me the lowdown on everything from trying to keep dust and dew off camp furniture to personal hygiene. 'When you go to the dunnies, love, make sure you take your own roll of dunny paper. No one leaves any there, and you don't want to go without.'

'That would be, er, shitty,' I said. Chook and Shirley cackled their heads off.

'If you want to do some washing, just bring it over here, Chook and me have got a little twin tub. It uses a full bucket for a wash. Got any washing powder?'

I shook my head. 'Nah, thanks, but I'll be right. A quick rinse down the river will do me.'

Shirley's forehead took on the texture of a sandstone cliff face. 'Salt isn't good for clothes. Rots the threads.'

Chook nodded gravely. 'Shirl's right. The salt buggers them up. They fall apart in no time.'

I shrugged. 'Maybe I will then.'

Shirley beamed back at me, 'Chook even made a clothesline that folds out from the side of the van. Didn't you love?'

'That's right. Everything you see here I done meself,' Chook told me, 'all the welding, anything like that. We haven't got the kind of money some of these bastards have got. Look at bloody Henderson over there. Hard to believe, isn't it?'

I followed his gaze to a massive caravan and tow vehicle combination some two or three hundred metres away, lights shining through from beneath what must have been a hydraulically operated awning. This behemoth could only be towed by what is known in the towing fraternity as a fifth wheel.

Really big vans have to be hitched onto a special towball on the vehicle tray, effectively moving the hitch point forward and therefore distributing the weight more evenly. I whistled. 'How much would a van like that be worth?'

'Just ask the wanker. He loves to skite about it. Two hundred and eighty grand, he reckons. The F250 is worth a hundred and twenty on its own. You can guarantee he's never done a hard day's work in his life. He's not a day under sixty-five, and his wife would be lucky to be thirty. She's a Filipina. Mail order bride.'

At another time I might have taken issue with the

racism underlying this comment, but I let it go. This was just good old-fashioned jealousy. Chook meant no harm. 'Nice bloke, though?'

'Nah, a blowhard.' Chook giggled to himself. 'Hates snakes. Had a python in the annexe one night and screamed like a sheila. Everyone thought there'd been a murder. Apparently the girl caught it by the tail and dragged it out while he jumped up and down on the bed, shitting himself.'

While the fish sizzled away, I got Chook's honest appraisal of the dozen or so vans within view. In Chook's opinion they were, in the main, overpriced, and owned by people with too much money for their own good. Bosses. Exploiters of honest workers.

'Half them bastards can't even back their van up properly. You should see them – having to get other blokes to do it for them. In my book a man's got to do things for himself. Where's the satisfaction in getting another bloke to drive your car? It's like getting him to service the missus for you.' He glared at me until I nodded my head in agreement.

A little dog scampered down the ladder steps, a fat silky terrier. He headed straight to a water bowl, took a few licks, then settled down on a folded blanket, resting his head on one paw, eyeing me warily the whole time. I wasn't a fan of small dogs, but at least this one didn't bark all the time or try to hump my leg.

'When we go back down south,' Chook told me while he levered the barra fillets off the plate, voice just starting to slur, 'I'm gonna weld meself up a new boat. Bigger than any of them mongrels have got. Just wait and see.'

On my way back to my camp that night I heard two men arguing in the distance, raised angry voices crackling across the still night. My senses went into overdrive, and my fists curled. I knew I had to ignore it. It was just hard, that's all.

I'd come here to heal. Getting involved in other people's fights was a bad idea.

I heard a cry of pain, then a shout. I stopped dead on the track, twitching like a rabbit. I stood there for perhaps five minutes. I didn't hear another sound. Finally, my shoulders dropping with relief, I turned back towards my camp.

I woke in the night only once, when a night breeze whistled through the casuarina needles, restless and arousing all at the same time, touching from soul to soul across the wild spaces of the north.

The ache inside me swelled and contracted like the tides, but it was the wind that soothed me. The firm ground and the silence. Here, where the dry leaves scuttled, and cane toads made a soft thud with each landing, there was a chance to heal. To fight the suspicion that there's no one else left. To lose this extreme kind of self-reliance where you trust no one except on the most basic level.

It's not the passage through the house of despair that does it to you, but the side rooms; the thick carpeted bedrooms. Cold kitchens. Dark closets. The people who loom out of the shadows on the way. The march of your feet in time with the clock on the lounge room wall. The things you have done, leaving memories like knives in the darkness, that visit you when your defences are lowest.

For an hour I lay with my chin on the base of my palm, prickled by the stubble on my cheek, until finally the feeling left me, and I was able to sleep, leaving the door of the house not closed, but banging lightly in the breeze.

Chapter Four

MAYOR DAVIS AND WALLABY YATES left camp with one of the two tandem trailers at dawn. I'd been awake for a while, warming my hands on a tin mug of coffee, savouring the aroma, watching the embers spit and flicker and listening to the birds waking over the river. I've always loved how the bush comes alive, not that it ever really sleeps.

First you hear the little stuff – wrens and finches darting around in the treetops – then a curlew settling down for the day. Nightshift over. Dayshift just beginning. A flight of magpie geese over the water. All this was soothing my heart when I heard the engine.

I stood up, stretching, slipping elastic sided boots on without socks. I walked closer in my track suit pants and woollen jumper, watching Yates back his Patrol up to one of the trailers, a covered twin-axle unit the size of a small pantech truck, streaked with red dust from drawbar to rear doors.

With Davis winding the jockey wheel, the trailer settled down onto the ball. I heard the clink of the safety chain as they secured it with the shackle. The two men drove away, slowly, keeping to the recommended speed. A supply run, I guessed, but it beat the hell out of me that the so-called mayor of Camp Leichhardt couldn't find himself better company for the drive.

Soon after sunrise I had the Stessl kicking up a clean wake as I motored upstream. Years earlier I had fished a series of deep pools up there – sunken logs creating abundant structure that attracted quality fish. The area was protected by a couple of shallow runs that tended to keep the regular fishermen out. Hauling boats up rocks and fast water was too much like hard work for most.

To pass the time I set up a route on the chartplotter – marking a deep-water path upriver. It was low tide, and a navigable channel now would be safe at any state of the tide. The morning sun was bright on the water and it was only my polarised sunnies that allowed me to pick out the swirl of a snag lurking under the current, or the edged pattern over the rim of a sandbar.

The water temperature was surprisingly low, even for July, sitting just below twenty-one Celsius. Borderline for barra. From my experience they'll still take a lure, but only if you swim it right past their nose, often more than once – annoy them into it. That means a lot of casting, trusting your gut, keeping on until your arm aches and self-doubt wears you down.

At the first of the cascades I motored right to left, looking for a channel, avoiding the white water. Small fish flitted away, dark shadows under the surface as I nosed upstream. Close to the southern bank I found the most consistent channel, still scarcely a metre deep, but enough for me to penetrate almost half way through before the deeper water ended in a shelf of rock, slick with benthic algae, reeking of earth and those age-old places rivers visit on their way to the sea.

You know the ones I mean – dark undercut banks, channels between drooping melaleucas and underwater sinkholes. Places where you understand how the original inhabitants dreamed up giant snakes and monsters, painting them on the sandstone ledges so they could share some of that power.

Here in the shallows, however, I had no choice but to cut and tilt the motor, throwing one foot over the gunnel, my neoprene boots secure on the gravel bottom. Taking the bow rope securely in one hand, I began to drag her up, hull scraping across the stones.

Heaving the boat through the rapids was a hard slog. Now and again the keel would catch on a protruding rock and need a good shove. Most of the time I trudged through knee-deep current, rope over my shoulder, sweating like a teamster.

My reward at the top was a clear, reflective pool, the tap-tap wing beat of rainbow bee eaters dusting the surface, and a crowd of flying foxes squabbling in the trees. I have seen these strange mammals so thick that the limbs drop with their weight, the crocs down below cleaning up the unfortunates as they tumble into the water, struggling for the bank in full knowledge of what their fate might be if they linger.

I've watched how the crocs swivel their heads sideways to make the capture, then tilt up to swallow the still-living, struggling flying fox whole, in two or three gulps, white teeth standing out in needle rows as the morsel goes down.

There was another set of rapids before I reached my spot, and this second was the longer and harder; four hundred metres of white water and side channels, truck sized boulders standing out in the stream, stained with the marks of ten thousand floods and white streaks from the cormorants and herons that hunted there or stood on the stone, drying their wings like sails.

Finally, sweating, but enjoying the work, I pushed the Stessl out into calm water and swung aboard. The waterhole beyond was pretty much how I remembered it, with short green grass between twisted old melaleuca trees, thick spongy roots holding the riverbank together.

Rather than starting the Honda, I dropped the Minn Kota electric motor into the water, using the foot control to steer it. The hull responded and I motored deeper into the pool, pleased to see structure on the sounder screen – sunken gums – deep below the surface. As the depth dropped down past six metres, the screen showed an unmistakeable bait school and even, once or twice, recognisable fish arches in the depths.

I motored to within casting range of a protruding snag, almost in the middle of the pool, before stopping again. This was, as far as barra are concerned, prime real estate.

Standing, I sent my first cast out towards the stub of old timber. This was just a preliminary move. Braided line casts better wet, and the first few throws were just to get things lubricated. By the third I had my distance, droplets of water flicking off the line in the sun as it arced out past the spot, the lure coming in slowly, rod tip low, close to the water surface.

The first few times I retrieved at a constant rate, then tried a few tricks – a dead stop here, a twitch there, even a genuine stutter that had worked wonders for me in the past. Still I persisted, sending twenty, thirty, or more casts into the area before I stopped, clipped on a deep diving lure and tried again.

The angle of retrieve changed now, the big-bladed Reidy's Taipan working deep with a dull, pulsing action that I felt through my arms and into my chest. There was a sudden change as it nudged up against an underwater log, and I stopped winding, letting its own buoyancy lift it away and prevent a snag.

I tried another dozen times but got no response. There was plenty more structure to try. Still hopeful, I laid down the rod and brought the Minn Kota back to life, motoring slowly to the next likely haunt.

Over three pleasant hours I poked upstream, hooking up once for a few exhilarating seconds.

Seventy or eighty centimetres of bright silver erupted through the water surface, gill covers flared to display the red flukes inside; a lure-rattling dance that ended with the lure flying back towards me through the air and the barra swimming free, back to the depths from where he had come.

I sat, hunched over in the boat, smiling like an idiot, knowing that in fishing, as in life, bad luck can easily dog a man, persisting until, somehow, he turns it around. On good days fish like that stick, and on bad days they don't. Not much point pondering or sitting around feeling blue. I gave myself a minute, then just got back on with it.

At around eleven I nosed into the bank for a cuppa from the thermos and a doze. I didn't hurry, getting back on the water an hour or so later, heading further upstream and negotiating yet another cascade, shorter and steeper than the last.

Rounding a bend, I was startled to see two Roper River locals on the bank, bare-chested, skin black as indigo in the morning light. At first I thought they were fishing, but instead of a friendly wave one shouted something to the other and retreated back from the riverbank, his mate close behind him.

Strange. I expected them to hang around for a chat, maybe give me a tip on where the bait schools were, where the big fish were feeding. Instead, within a few moments they had disappeared, as if I had imagined the whole thing.

Intent on confirming that I wasn't dreaming, I motored across, hopped out onto the bank and pulled the Stessl up behind me. There, in the muddy patches between the paperbark roots I saw fresh footprints. My mind had not been playing tricks on me.

I saw something else, too – a long indentation in the mud where something had been on the bank – similar to the slide mark of a small croc, but too smooth, too regular. I bent to my knees, wondering what the hell I was looking at, then turned and stared at the scrub into which the men had disappeared.

No point in giving chase. If they didn't want to be found then I'd be unlikely to get near them. Shrugging the incident away I stepped back into the boat and pushed off. I must have startled them, I decided. Maybe they were just teenagers and I gave them a shock.

Still, as I began the long drift downstream, casting as I went, the incident sucked the pleasure from the day in the same way as a niggling toothache. In fact, the fishing no longer seemed as urgent and important as it had that morning.

Chapter Five

MAYOR DAVIS AND WALLABY YATES returned before dusk. I couldn't resist checking out what they had brought back in the trailer, so I walked down the track until I had a better view, standing with my hands clenched in the pockets of my moleskins. They parked next to one of three shipping containers and threw open the doors. Terry Yates, the other brother, appeared from a rundown old van nearby and began the unloading.

Beer. Carton after green carton of Victoria Bitter cans stacked on pallets. Having nothing better to do I wandered closer and counted, losing my way at fifty cases. I was so engrossed that I didn't notice Chook Fowler come up until he was right beside me.

'How ya going?' he asked.

'Yeah, good, and you?'

'Good, mate, good.'

'That's a shitload of beer,' I observed.

'Yeah. And they'll be back for more in a few weeks.'

'You lot don't drink that much, surely?'

Chook shrugged, and glanced at me nervously. 'You get fish today?'

'Just catfish. One hook-up on a nice barra but he spat the lure back at me. You do any good?'

'Didn't put the boat in the water. Chucked a sickie.' He laughed at his own joke. I had a feeling he'd used it before.

While we talked, the trailer unloading ceased and the container doors slammed shut. The trailer was backed into its place and unhitched. Now the Nissan headed around the track directly for us. Chook stepped nervously off the path but I stood my ground, watching them come. The two Yates boys occupied the front seats. Both were drinking. Stopping in front of me Wallaby wound down the window, forearm resting on the sill, beer stubby held towards me so I could see white foam on the interior of the brown bottle, and the faded print on the stubby holder. 'Hey, cop,' he said, lip twisting unpleasantly, 'what are you staring at?'

'Oh, nothing, just having a chat to my friend Chook, here.'

He turned on my new mate, 'Fowler, you'd be best off choosing your friends a little more wisely, or me and you are gonna have a chat. Got it?'

Chook said nothing, but I could see from his expression that they scared him. That annoyed me. Nomads like Chook came here to fish and relax, not to get bullied by amateur standover men.

I advanced to the car window, and Wallaby Yates took a long swig of his beer, a portion of which dribbled down along the fuzz on either side of his lips. He scowled at me. 'I thought we told you to piss off.'

'Yes, you did.'

'So?'

'So nothing. Leave me alone, and,' I jabbed a finger at Chook Fowler, still standing uncertainly a few paces away, 'leave him alone.'

'Or what?'

I said nothing, just turned back to catch Chook's eye. I know that he wanted me to keep pushing, but I had gone as far as I could. This was not what I needed, not now, and yet to show weakness was to let the bastards win.

Terry Yates turned to his brother and they laughed. 'Yellow, are you? You better be packed up and gone by morning, or yer gonna regret it.'

'I'm terrified,' I said, voice dripping with sarcasm. It was the best I could do and, in any case, the short conversation seemed to have exhausted Yates's stock of empty phrases and emptier threats, because he shouted a single expletive and hit the pedal, stirring up such a quantity of dust that I'm sure his friend Davis would have disapproved.

Chapter Six

I FISHED DOWNSTREAM the next morning, tucking myself into a creek entrance and working the snags repeatedly. Anyone who thinks barra fishing is easy needs to see just how frustrating it can be when the bloody things won't cooperate. Even here in some of the richest water in the world it can be a struggle.

Of course, there are times when it is easy. When the creeks are running turbid brown after the wet, mangrove and reed lined channels between the flood plains thick with bait, it's possible to score fish after fish, woofing up lures or live baits like there's no tomorrow.

That morning, however, frustration started to build. Perhaps it was a throwback to primitive times, when a hunter was judged on his ability to bring home a feed, but non-anglers have no idea just how much of an angler's self-esteem is tied up in his ability to catch fish.

I tried swimbaits, soft vibes, even a surface lure or two. I did my best to stay positive – watching the water for signs of underwater action through my sunnies – placing the lure deep into structure. I kept it free of weed and swimming right, changing brands and types as conditions permitted. Even a long session with soft plastics failed to produce the goods.

I was working a likely looking snag in the middle morning – a newly fallen tree with branches that covered two hundred square metres of water. I'd noticed some fish arches showing on the sounder, and was braced for a strike when I heard the growl of a two-stroke outboard motor approaching from around the bend.

I turned to look, annoyed. Ever since I switched over to four-strokes, silent and sweet, the racket of old technology motors gets on my nerves. This one was travelling fast. I braced myself for the bow wave and noise, trying not to feel pissed off at what the passing vessel might do to my prospects.

Finally, long after I first heard it, the boat came around the bend, a big old punt like the pros use, wide in the beam and with unusually high freeboard. Wallaby Yates was perched up in the bows, staring straight ahead. Terry, in the stern, had his pink left hand on the tiller arm of an old blue band Mercury outboard, from which a cloud of smoke emanated.

What really caught my attention, however, was

the lack of fishing rods. Instead, a canvas-wrapped bundle dominated the centreline, almost as tall as a man and obviously heavy, for the hull sat low in the water. As I watched, the motor faltered and the boat started towards me.

Even as I prepared myself for whatever confrontation was to come, I was surprised to hear raised voices, then the engine blaring again and the boat turning away from me, continuing downstream. For some reason they had changed their minds about coming over to have a go at me.

I stared after the craft and its mysterious cargo as it faded into the distance, trailed by a blue plume of smoke. Only once the waves it left behind had ceased smashing into the bank did I cast again, my mind busy – troubled by what I had just seen.

Two hours later I had moved downstream about a mile, taking considerable care stalking my way up to a patch of snags, motoring in with the electric. Now that the sun was high, I switched to a deep diver, working it maybe three metres down, with every trick in the book – twitches, stops and pulses.

I had just settled into the rhythm when I heard the unholy racket of that punt as it blared back upstream. Now the canvas-covered load was gone, and I could see the Yates boys clearly, grinning when they saw me, the hull deviating my way.

The Mercury roared, and I stopped mid retrieve

as it struck me that they were now moving very fast, and directly towards me. Fifty metres. Thirty. White water licked around the bow as the punt gained more speed.

I dropped the rod and settled into the seat, reaching for the starter rope. The pricks, it seemed, were going to ram me.

'You bloody idiots!' I shouted, but still the punt bored on. It was heavier and more solid that my Stessl. I had no doubts as to who would come off worse if they struck.

I pulled the starter, knowing it was already too late. They were almost on me. I grabbed the throttle with my hand even as the Honda purred into life.

Now, within reach of my boat, Terry Yates heaved the tiller across, and turned sharply away. By then I was also moving, but both courses of action were too late to prevent some contact. The blunt end of the punt scraped the paint from a section of my bow, rocking the hull.

I heard their maniacal laughter, then tasted a blast of two-stroke smoke as they accelerated again.

'Fuckwits!' I called, twisting the throttle back into neutral before I hit a snag. But the combined wake was rocking my tinnie madly and I was forced to hold on or be thrown overboard. By the time it had stabilised they had rounded the bend back towards Camp Leichhardt.

Later, back at camp, I was in an evil mood. I ate alone, thick droughtmaster T-bone, topped with tinned mushrooms, served al fresco at the camp table, gas lamp burning, listening to the distant, subdued sounds of camp life from the vans – televisions, music and people talking on their mobile phones.

Dishes done, I checked the fire, moving a few burning logs away from the edges. Satisfied, I stood up and strode from the camp. I had known ever since I reached the boat ramp that I couldn't let the events of the day ride. It was time to pay the brothers a visit.

I walked down the track towards the Yates boys and their crappy old Regal van. I'd seen their Nissan parked there, not far from the shipping containers. I strode past Mayor Davis who sat alone in his camp chair, warming his hands over a tidy campfire.

The Yates boys, when I reached their van, were also outside, with a near-dead fire putting out more smoke than heat. They each sat in a cheap BCF folding chair, with empty stubbies scattered around.

Wallaby Yates looked up at me and giggled insanely. 'What do you want?'

Terry tried to stand up, but he fell sideways, knocking the chair over. After a comedy routine that ended with him crawling over to the Nissan and using the bull bar to pull himself up, he spat in my direction.

'It's the fucking cop. What are you gonna do, arrest us for breathing?'

They were drunk, off their stupid faces. It was like talking to zombies. I turned away, striding back to camp. Davis called out to me as I passed but I ignored him.

I felt like I was no longer on holidays, but back in Katherine. Picking up third-generation alcoholics. Handcuffing twenty-year-old men who try to fight like warriors yet live the lives of sick, alcohol-dependent old men.

I know what the grog can do, believe me. Because it did it to me too.

I unrolled my swag and went to sleep with a heavy heart. Still angry. Still hurting.

Chapter Seven

IF DAVIS WAS the unofficial mayor of Camp Leichhardt; Ian Henderson in the giant Wildcat caravan was the rich magnate. As if to prove his interest in the little people, he sent out an invitation for me to visit, the next afternoon. I was tying a bimini twist, a complex fishing knot at which I'm no expert, using a tree as an assistant and utilising one foot as well as my hands. My plan was to run down to the river mouth the following day and have a crack at pelagic fish out to sea. Mixing things up sometimes helps, and the weather forecast was for five to ten knot sou'easters and seas under a metre.

The voice that startled me was soft and polite. Looking up I was surprised to see a young woman standing in my camp. She was drop-dead gorgeous, so much so that I lost my composure and tripped over myself, losing my grip on the knot in the process. This accident forced me to swear in a way I would not normally have done in the presence of a lady. I expected a rebuke, but when I looked up she was laughing at me, and I couldn't help but smile back.

'Hi,' she said. 'My name is Malea.'

'Hi. I'm Ben.' I realised that she must be Hendo's young wife, the woman that Chook had dismissed as a mail order bride. I was stunned, I hadn't expected her to be quite so glamorous. She was Eurasian in appearance, with dark hair to the small of her back, almond eyes and slender limbs.

'I have an invitation for you,' she said, 'from my husband, Ian. He would like you to come over for a drink this evening.'

'Yeah, well, thank you. Only I don't drink.'

'Oh, Ian knows that, he will be happy to offer you something soft. I don't drink either. Well, only champagne.'

I laughed. 'That's kind of not drinking, isn't it? Do you mind if I ask what brought this on – why your husband wants me to come over?'

Malea shrugged those finely-shaped shoulders. 'Ian has heard about you from some of the others. He wants to meet you.'

'Fair enough. What time do you want me?'

'Around four o'clock. Is that suitable?'

'Of course. I'll see you then.'

With a toss of her head sending ripples of light across that glossy black hair, she sauntered back towards the Wildcat, leaving me a little amused, a touch more curious, and dealing with a very real and instant attraction.

The Wildcat was a beast of a caravan, though I got no further than the annexe, floored with interlocking foam sheets, and decked out like a covered courtyard in a rich family home. Extra rooms popped up and out from the main body of the van, increasing the overall size to that of a standard Territory donga. A fridge sat on a pallet, and beside it a selection of those stacking tray modules full of clothes and practical bits and pieces like pegs, rope, barbecue tools and torches.

Hendo was a shortish man, with a driving confidence. His grip was firm and dry when we shook hands, and his gaze direct. There were few wrinkles on his face, tucked away in the corners of his eyes and forehead. Chook had estimated the man's age as around sixty-five, though he looked younger, and I wondered if a Botox-wielding plastic surgeon had touched him up at some stage. His eyes were a little *too* direct, set in a permanent stare.

'Pleased to meet you,' he said. 'I've heard a lot about you.'

Yeah, I thought to myself, a cop who doesn't drink, can't catch fish ... all the juicy stuff that becomes gossip-worthy in a closed community such as this. I looked around. 'This is one hell of a caravan.'

'Oh yeah, it'd want to be good for the dollars I paid for it. Took me months to make my mind up – there's a lot of choice out there, even in this price bracket.' He chuckled. 'Had the dealers falling all over themselves. Shoulda seen the poor bastards when I put down a deposit – had them shaking like schoolgirls.'

Malea came through the doorway with a plate in one hand, closed the screen door behind her and sat the plate delicately on the table in front of us – rice crackers and cheese. As she came close her fragrance hit me like a sledgehammer, and my eyes were drawn to her. I couldn't keep them away as she brought me a can of lemon squash.

'Would you like a glass for that?' she asked.

'No thanks, I'll take it as it comes.'

With a nod and a smile, she took a champagne flute from a shelf beside the fridge, and carried a bottle to Hendo to open, a task he accomplished without fuss. This achieved, Malea lifted her glass, took a delicate little sip, and then perched on the chair, one perfect leg drawn up, bare foot on the seat.

'So how's the fishing going?' Hendo asked.

'Not too good, so far. But I enjoy it anyway. Always do. What about you?'

I'd noticed a knock-out fibreglass boat out beside the van, a Haines Prostrike with a ridiculous amount of horsepower on the transom. The gel coat was glaring white with dark blue pinstripes, and the interior decked out with plush pedestal chairs, a casting platform and grey marine carpet. A sounder/chartplotter combo the size of a small television sat atop the console. I wondered if they actually caught fish in the rig. Looked too damn nice to put in the water.

'I personally haven't been out for a week or two,' Ian told me, placing one arm possessively around Malea's shoulder. 'The little wife is the gun fisherwoman. Loves it.'

Opening the can of squash, I took a sip and smiled at her, partly to share my discomfort at Henderson calling her 'the little wife,' partly because among my other faults I have a weakness for fishing females. 'Really?'

A glimpse of small, white teeth. 'I've always enjoyed fishing. Since I was a little girl. My father used to take me.'

'Good on you. Maybe you could teach me a thing or two.'

'I'm sure I couldn't teach you anything ...'

Again she changed position, crossing her legs, one foot on her knee, showing off neatly manicured toenails and a gold chain around one ankle. I wondered how the hell she kept her feet so clean in this dustbowl of a camp. I had to consciously stop my eyes from roving further, snapping them back to the much less interesting Hendo.

'I hear you're a cop,' he said.

I almost yawned. This was getting tiresome. 'Yeah, up in Katherine.'

'But you're here on holiday, right?'

'Yep. Just fishing ... having a rest.'

'Nice change, hey?'

'Sure.'

Hendo planted his hands on his knees in the manner of a man about to deliver a lecture. 'The problem is that magistrates and judges let crooks off scot-free. Slap 'em on the wrist and send 'em away to do the same again. Gaols are like bloody holiday camps. The law needs balls, like it used to have, years ago.' He held his hands out, palms up, as if cupping a pair of imaginary testicles.

I had heard these sentiments a thousand times before. I could have told him what Berrimah Prison was really like, what Sixty Minutes style documentaries don't show about life inside – how soul destroying being locked in a room could be. Yet what was the point? The man was opinionated and unlikely to welcome contradiction. Instead, I took a long swig of lemon squash and avoided staring at Malea.

'How long are you planning on staying?' Hendo asked.

'A week, maybe more. Until I get some fish.'

He appeared to consider this, leaning back in the seat and giving his stubby some attention. He intrigued me. He didn't appear to be into fishing, and why else would a man spend three or four months in a place like this? The money for the van and F250 came from somewhere. I wanted to know where, and had nothing to lose by asking. 'You've obviously made some money,' I said. 'What line of work were you in?'

'I'm what the newspapers call an entrepreneur,' he smiled. 'Mainly property developing. Made a killing. Got in and out of the stock market at the right time too.'

'Lucky you.' If the sarcasm in my voice was obvious, I wasn't too bothered. Okay, I had asked for it, but I found rich men's stories of how they got rich tedious, and this one was no exception.

He must have caught on, for something changed in his face. To say that the mask slipped summed it up. All the light went out of his expression, revealing only the mean, hard core underneath. Even his body language changed, folding his arms. 'There's plenty of other rivers – why don't you go down the Gulf a bit. I heard the Limmen's fishing well at the moment.'

This was a polite version of the Yates boys', 'Why don't you get the fuck out of here' speech. I aped his body language, folding my own arms. 'You don't like cops either, I take it.'

'That's not true. It's just that – people are here to

relax – you're making everyone nervous.'

I looked at the smarmy, arrogant little prick and realised that he was making me twice as angry as the Yates boys had. They had the excuse of being stupid. This bloke was just an arsehole.

'Why?' I asked. 'Have you got something to hide?'

'No. But I don't want you here.'

I decided that next time I went camping I'd tell everyone that I was a plumber, or a dentist. For the first time since I had arrived, I considered doing exactly what he had just suggested, pulling up stumps and pissing off somewhere away from Hendo and the Yates boys, the Nomads and their satellite dishes, their baby dogs and intrigues.

Looking up I met Malea's eyes and it was as if she read my mind. There was something knowing in that look and I realised that there was more to her than met the eye, a lot more than the 'mail order bride' Chook Fowler had dismissed her as.

'I'm not going anywhere,' I told Hendo. 'This is a public place, and I don't really give a shit if you like me being here or not. You or your mates.'

Hendo squared his shoulders as if trying to show me that he had brawn as well as brain. 'Suit yourself. This is a free country. Sort of.'

I stood up, drained my can and crushed it in one hand, before placing it ever so gently on the table. It was a show-off thing to do, and a bit pathetic, but I had to do something. I turned to Malea. 'Thank you for your hospitality.'

The apology was in her eyes, shame at what her man was like. I looked back down at Hendo. 'See you later.' I would have liked to add the word dickhead, but there was no point in a declaration of war.

If I had to take these blokes head on, the less they knew about my intentions the better.

Back at my camp I settled down to a quiet meal of snags and spuds, finished off with a giant slice of apple pie Shirley sent over. I was determined to be on the river early the next morning. The less time I spent in this insane camp, I decided, the better off I would be.

Chapter Eight

DAWN ON A TOP END RIVER is one of the side benefits of my sport that few people apart from anglers ever know. The smell is complex and intoxicating, a mix of flying fox urine, heady blossoms, and the river water itself, deep and inviting. I inhaled this mixture like a drug and idled downstream, unwilling to open the throttle right up and break the spell.

There was always something to see – a diving cormorant surfacing with his catch beside a snag, a croc having a peek at me before slinking back below the surface and away – a sea eagle or brahminy kite swooping low over the water or picking his prey to bits in the high branches of a dead tree. Once or twice, seeing a school of pop-eye mullet breaking the surface, I cut the motor and peppered the area with casts, but whatever had been chasing them was not to be tempted.

I motored about six miles downstream, stopping

finally at a snag-filled reach of river that looked promising. I cut the motor and drifted with the ebb, working over every bit of structure I could find. Fine mist was still ghosting off the surface and I felt confident. It looked so good. Something had to happen.

Even so, I was prepared to be patient. Sometimes you have to be like that. After an hour without a touch I changed lures, then every ten minutes after that. A Panic Stations vibe, then a gold bomber; a barra classic, and finally; a Halco minnow in Qantas colours.

Persistence. There lay the key, surely. The fish were quiet, inactive, but all I had to do was run one past the nose of a fish and he'd strike. Sooner or later it would happen.

Around nine I heard an outboard, yet quiet and subdued. A four-stroke. A boat appeared upriver and powered towards me. The Haines Signature Prostrike. That gorgeous fibreglass hull.

I don't know which I recognised first, the beautiful boat or the beautiful woman at the wheel, but by then she had seen me too, and slowed up. It was Malea, dressed in khaki shorts and shirt, polarised sunglasses a stripe across her face.

'Good morning,' she called.

'Hi.'

'I wondered if I would see you down here.'

'Yes.'

'Any fish?'

'No, not a touch so far.' I wished I had something to show off, preferably bright silver and a metre long.

'Do you want to tag along with me? I know a spot that's fishing well at the moment.'

I shrugged. 'I can't do any worse.'

Malea turned those sunglasses-covered eyes onto me, looking like an advertisement for everything from lipstick to Kathmandu shirts. Her black hair was tied back into a ponytail, and if anything it accentuated the fine structure of her face. 'I'm glad I saw you, Ben, I wanted to apologise for my husband. He was rude to you.'

'Don't worry about it.'

'No. He was being an asshole.'

I noticed that she said asshole, the American way, instead of arsehole, and to me that made it a little less of an insult, more of a joke. Searching her face, I couldn't tell if she said it with feeling or not.

'Come on then,' she urged. 'I want to fish.'

I stowed my rods into the upright holders and pulled the starter so the Honda bubbled away in idle. 'Ready when you are.'

Malea took off at speed. The Haines was fast, and the GPS showed twenty-eight knots when I settled back a hundred metres behind her, tracking in the calm in the middle of her wake.

I had mixed feelings, I had to admit. The fishing

had been frustrating, sure, but deep in some old-fashioned core of me I resented having this young, gorgeous woman showing me where to fish. After all, I had grown up here in the north and spent much of my childhood and youth on the Roper, the Victoria, the Adelaide, and the Daly. I'd caught maybe a dozen fish over the one metre benchmark. I knew my camp craft, could navigate by the stars and feed myself on billy goat plum and water lily tubers if I had to. A bushman by any measure. This young thing was presuming to show me a thing or two, and it rankled.

There was another source of unease. Malea was one hell of a nice chick. I liked her a lot. Could easily like her too much. I had come here to relieve some stress, but heading off into the wilds with another man's wife was not the most relaxing pastime. I wondered if it might lead to the kind of trouble I had come here to escape.

Malea led me downstream for ten or so minutes before a mangrove island loomed ahead. There she cut the motor and waited for me. 'It's very shallow around here,' she called, 'you'll have to tilt the motor up to get through.'

I said nothing, but did as she suggested, using the power trim to get the prop up out of the mud as we approached the shallow side of the island. The area did not look, at first glance, suitable for fishing. I saw mangrove stubs on the bottom, and big mullet leaving ripples and a turbid cloud as they pulsed away across the flats. A mud crab the size of a dinner plate scooted sideways, spooked at our approach.

At this stage Malea stopped, took her rods out of the holders and laid them flat along the deck. I followed suit, still confused as to where she was intending to take me. This water just didn't seem to go anywhere.

Then we were into the mangroves themselves, well behind the island, and a channel not much wider than the boat. The outboard skeg, tilted as it was, struck mud constantly, leaving a churned up trail of dirty water behind us. The channel went on and on.

Miraculously, it opened out, gradually at first, and then reverse-funnelled into a genuine lagoon, studded with water lilies and sunken timber, maybe five or six hectares in extent. The prop ran free, and I tilted the motor down so it could bite better in this deeper water. Malea pulled up, obviously enjoying the stunned surprise on my face. 'The depth in here is just a few metres and the water temperature is warmer than the main river. I've done quite well here, lately.'

'How the hell did you find it?'

'Google Earth. Ian has the pro version and sometimes I have a play with it.'

'Well done.'

'Would you like to tie your boat up and join me?

It'll be more fun to fish together.'

'Yeah, if you want me to.'

'Fishing is so much better when you've got someone with you, don't you think?'

I wasn't sure. Under most circumstances I'm probably happier alone, but then I'd never had someone who looked like her to fish with. 'Just give me a minute to get organised.' Motoring over to a substantial snag, I made the bow rope fast. When Malea came alongside I passed over my rods, tackle box, and a small cooler that contained sandwiches, biscuits and drinks. This done, I stepped from hull to hull, both being so remarkably stable that they shifted only a little as I did so.

Settling into the bow seat, I smiled at her. Up close, she was simply stunning, her legs brown and athletic, skin with a lustre I don't think I'd ever quite seen before. By climbing onto that boat I was aware that I was already doing something dangerous, but Malea did not appear to think so, and besides, no one would ever see us here.

With an expert hand on the tiller, Malea motored further into the lagoon, the Yamaha scarcely ticking over. A grey heron on the bank gave us an irate honk and broke into an ungainly run, beating his wings as he went, finally getting airborne at the water's edge. One or two ducks paddled away. A mozzie landed on my forearm and I slapped at it, leaving a smear of blood on my skin.

Finally, without saying a word, Malea switched off the ignition, and pointed at the Minn Kota, by which I understood that she wanted it in the water. I leaned over, released the clip, and lowered the skeg. Then, standing, I lifted one of my rods and unclipped the hooks from a runner. Malea was doing the same. I noted her gear. Loomis rods and Chronarch reels. Nothing but the best.

A lot of southerners and youngsters use eggbeater reels these days, but I am a purist. Baitcasters are, to me, the mark of someone who knows how to fish. I had to put Malea in this category.

My first cast was a loosener, but even so I felt the change here. The water was charged as if with an electric current. Insect life everywhere. Archer fish chopping at the surface. Swirls. Spider webs intricately spun, billowing between tree trunks like silk parachutes.

Malea fished in silence, and I gave thanks for that. I hate chattering anglers. Silence is part of the attraction, part of this world, and the noisy often miss clues and nuances that reward the listener; the observer.

The lure, a shallow runner, black and green, wiggled its way back to me, just shy of the surface. Having almost reached the boat a silver flash appeared from nowhere, not touching the lure, but visible nonetheless, leaving a disturbed surge on the surface. I dragged the rod tip sideways, trying to entice a strike, but with no luck. I turned to Malea, intent on her own cast, and mouthed, 'I had a follow. First cast.' She smiled encouragingly, and I went back to work, picking out a floating pandanus frond half draped on a protruding snag, sending the lure a few metres past it, cranking quickly for a few turns before dropping back the pace, twitching a few times ...

Hook-up. Shit. Second cast in this strange, magical place. This was no small fish, not bothering with the usual leap, but instead a headlong dive for cover that saw it tearing line against serious drag.

'Hey, well done,' Malea encouraged from behind me, but I was intent on thumbing the spool and trying to get some control over the fish. I heard the electric outboard whirr as she motored us gently sideways, giving me some angle to work with. I felt the stretched tension as the braid touched sunken timber and I swore under my breath. I could still feel the fish, but there was a rubbing sensation between us, indicating that somewhere down there my fish had wrapped me tight around structure.

Freespooling the reel is an old trick that sometimes works, letting the fish think she is free and encouraging her to swim back out of her underwater maze. I kept a thumb on the spool, ready to apply pressure if needed, but let the line go completely limp. Thirty seconds, then a minute, passed. Hoping. This was only my second hook-up of the trip. I needed this one.

Finally, instinct telling me it was time, I began to wind, taking up the slack line until the pressure came on again. This was make or break time. I lifted the rod tip and gave it every ounce of pressure I could exert without pulling hooks or mangling split rings. To my relief and pleasure the fish came with me, no trace of the previous external pressure.

'We're in the clear,' I grunted, and this time I gave the fish no chance to re-enter its hideaway. I used my thumb like a vice, grudging every metre of run. Up close to the boat I couldn't stop another ten-metre surge, but managed to put the brakes on, just shy of the timber.

Tiring now, the fish let me lead her towards the boat. Coming up beside the gunwale she was magnificent. A metre from nose to tail, silver in her scaled suit of armour, eyes shining orange back up at me. Truly the queen of Australian sport fish. All the mystery and beauty of the North in one ancient, perfectly adapted package.

Malea netted her for me, and together we lifted the fish onto the carpeted deck. While my companion took a dozen snaps with her phone I worked the treble hooks out. The broad tail padded hard against the carpeted deck.

'What a beauty,' Malea said.

One hand under her belly and the other around her tail fin, I lifted her over the side and pushed her nose first back into the water. At first nothing happened, but then with a pulse of that tail she drove down and away, almost lazily.

I looked back up at Malea, grinning like a mad bastard.

'You let her go,' she said.

'The first one,' I explained, 'I always let the first one go. Family tradition.' People who don't fish will never understand this – the relationship between hunter and prey. For him (or her) to eat, a fish must die, perhaps more than one, but the angler knows his place in the food web more than most – that his fate is linked with the species he chooses to pursue.

After ten minutes of probing casts, Malea hooked up also, landing a feisty eighty-centimetre beauty that she kept for the table. I followed up with one of my own, just a few centimetres over legal size that would give up delicious, pan-sized fillets later.

Close to noon, we tied the boat up on a grassy bank and ate our lunches, picnicking like old friends, full of a sense of privilege at the spirit of this place and being fortunate to hunt and partake of the creatures that inhabited it. I am no dab hand at sandwiches, but I ate hungrily. I dusted the crumbs from my legs and swigged enough water to drown a cat.

'How did you meet Hendo?' I asked finally. Malea was sitting on a towel, legs drawn half up, hair tied back loosely. The question was begging to be asked. Why would someone like you be with someone like him?

Her smile never faltered, but for the first time since we met her eyes took on a defensive, if not to say protective, glimmer. 'That,' she said softly, 'is none of your business.'

I could have slapped myself for being a fool. God, I hardly knew her, had no right to ask a question like that. 'Of course not,' I said, 'sorry. Shouldn't have asked.' Once a cop, always a cop. Can't help the curiosity, the questions. To hide my discomfort I stood, stiff from the boat and sitting. 'Might stretch the legs for a minute.'

'Of course.' She stood, smiling as if to reassure me that there were no hard feelings – that we were still good with each other – then shook off the towel and crushed it under her arm. 'And then I'll finish showing you how to catch fish.'

I grinned back. 'Looking forward to it.'

We ambled along the bank of the lagoon, trying to recapture the friendship I'd felt before I asked my dumb question. I think we were both trying hard, but there was a new awkwardness between us. As if to kill the silence I pointed out tracks on the damp ground at the lagoon's edge, and the animals they belonged to. Wallaby. Dingo. Ibis. Up ahead a good-sized croc ambled into the water with a splash, holding station a few metres out, watching us through those armour-plated mounds that sheltered his eyes.

I watched respectfully as we walked past, and had scarcely travelled on another twenty metres when I stopped dead at a strange sight on the lagoon bank up ahead. Someone had gone to a lot of trouble to cut two cypress logs, and set them into the bank, leaning at an angle out from the bank. These were, in turn, fixed to uprights with expert 'Cobb and Co' fencing wire ties. The structure was not designed for longevity, but to facilitate the rapid loading and unloading of something from a small boat.

'What the hell's that for?' I wondered aloud. Malea shrugged, but kept pace with me as I strode quickly to the spot.

The structure was no more than what it seemed, yet the galvanised wire had not yet rusted. It was a recent construction.

'Maybe someone camped here,' Malea said, 'wanted an easy way of keeping their boat in the water.'

That explanation had occurred to me; it seemed like the most reasonable possibility. But why would someone do that much work for a mere campsite?

I was about to start walking back towards the

boat when I spotted something unusual in the grass. Something small and black. I squatted down and picked it up between thumb and forefinger. It was a black plastic tool with a spike on one side and a hex head grip on the other, no thicker than a pencil, and shorter than my little finger.

'Now what the hell is that?'

Malea stepped closer, craning her neck to look. 'No idea.' I put the thing in my pocket and she looked at me strangely. 'Aren't you supposed to be on holidays?'

I knew what she was really saying: why the hell don't you stop worrying about everything and everybody and enjoy yourself?

It was a bloody good question. I wish I knew the answer.

Chapter Nine

THE ROPER BAR store was a fifty-minute drive up the track. After recovering from shock at the price of diesel, I filled the tanks, then bought supplies inside, waiting behind half a dozen Roper women lined up with basket loads of groceries, the kids running amok between the corridors and outside, snot nosed and smiling, dark skin glowing. One little girl hid between her mother's legs, peeping out at me, smiling, hamming it up with a natural theatrical instinct.

The Engel fridge brimming with fresh milk, butter and fruit, I drove another half hour on dirt roads through Mara, and finally Gajiyuma, an Aboriginal township of around five hundred people. This was a dry community, with signs at the borders proclaiming a liquor free area. The area immediately before the restricted zone was littered with thousands of discarded alcohol containers. Acres of them. Wine casks, bladders, bottles and cans. Plastic bags, old drums. Enough rubbish to keep a recycling depot busy for a year.

The settlement occupied the slopes and summit of a hill, falling away to the river some distance away. It was typical of larger indigenous communities. Housing ranged from older, often abandoned or burned-out prefabricated dwellings the size of Wahroonga or Toorak bathrooms. Amongst them were newer, elevated homes, some well-kept. Abandoned cars lay everywhere, along with camp dogs, so coated with cattle ticks that they shone in the sunlight.

You cannot judge an Indigenous community with Southern eyes, because you are looking through the filter of comparative privilege into what was and remains another culture. You are looking at a culture caught in the jaws of change. Yes, they have no tradition of picking up rubbish.

For fifty thousand years you dropped that mussel shell or bone when you have finished with it and soon enough a dog, or a bird, or ants, will take care of the rest. Now, however, the rubbish dropped is not bone and shell, but plastic and foil. The communities have grown into towns, and cannot cope with the numbers of people. Their waste. The rubbish.

White nurses teach mothers to use disposable nappies on their babies rather than holding them up over a bush. You see the result – soiled nappies blown up against the low chain-mesh fences that surround the buildings.

You see that there is no running water to a house. The women have carried water as their mothers did before them and it does not faze them. Extended family groups still go out bush and get tucker.

You see the starving camp dogs and you wonder why no one looks after them. You don't understand that you are seeing not a master-servant scenario like in North Ryde, Logan or Glenside, but a complex, symbiotic relationship that goes back at least ten thousand years. These people will rarely pull ticks off the dogs, nor take them to the non-existent vet. Occasionally they might throw the odd bone for them to fight over. You think this is cold. But this is not your world. It is theirs.

People change, over time. Expectations change. But so many times I have seen white noses wrinkle in distaste at what are so often termed primitive conditions. Third world conditions. Strip away the houses, the grog, and the crowded dwellings, and you have a people perfectly adapted to their natural landscape, trying to do what they have always done, only they can't, because Uncle who showed the boys how to hunt is drunk in Katherine with a five-year life expectancy. Auntie who once dug for mussels in the mud is with him; singing for him when he fights, crying over him when he falls, bearing children she does not have the focus to raise, so that they become the responsibility of extended family, or often, an overwhelmed Department of Health and Community Services.

Washing machines. Why? Clothes are a white man's requirement in any case. Wash dishes? There is no tradition of hygiene. It wasn't necessary. Toilet paper? Would a man carry a roll everywhere he walks? Of course not.

White society has brought many things these people did not need or want. Worst of all they brought grog. Cask wine. Beer. Banned from the community itself, but it is there on the fringes. A toxic tide lapping at an island.

I stopped outside the cop station. It was built like a brick shithouse, with bars over the windows and a door that would stop a battering ram. I knew the sergeant here – Chris Reilly. He'd been out here for nearly five years – well and truly a full tour of duty in this part of the world.

Stepping into the entry, I closed the door, and the roar of the generator faded to a hum. I fronted the counter with its blast of frigid air from the air conditioner. I rang the bell and Chris appeared, a naked baby in his arms. It took him a few seconds to recognise me, but then I hadn't shaved for a couple of days, and we hadn't met up for a while.

He knew me though. They all did. I was famous in a way. I was famous for one thing, and it wasn't something I liked to remember.

'Ben, isn't it? Ben Mulligan?' He patted the baby's back gently.

'That's it.'

He smiled. 'Man, it's nice to have one of the boys down here.' Still without letting go of the kid he unclipped a waist-high gate in the counter and let me through. 'Come in and have a cuppa. What the hell are you doing here?'

'Holiday. A bit of fishing down at Camp Leichhardt.'

'Yeah, with all the wrinklies, huh?' Chris's stiff little blonde moustache twitched when he laughed.

We went out the back door of the station and across to one of two police residences, still inside the same compound. This building was constructed no less strongly than the station itself, also barred on the windows and with solid security doors. Communities like Gajiyuma could, and occasionally did, erupt.

In spite of the blockhouse façade, however, someone had made an attempt with the garden. A bougainvillea was the highlight, climbing over and around an archway made of two-inch poly pipe over steel pickets.

Chris led me through the front door and into the

living room of the house, strewn with the paraphernalia of a young family – cardboard nappy boxes, a change table, a bouncer. The TV was on and a young woman looked up as I came in. She was about thirty, and pretty, but with lank, sweat-stained hair and a thin smile. She stood up and we shook hands. Her face was pale, as if she never went outside into the sun.

'Cuppa tea?'

'Yeah, thanks.'

'How do you have it, love?'

'No sugar and a dash of milk, please.' Settling onto the lounge I waited for Chris to do the same. 'No offsider?'

'Yeah, young Indigenous bloke by the name of Eric Swanson. A good kid. He's in court in Katherine. Took a paddy wagon full with him.'

That was normal. These bush stations generally had to clear the cells out and take the prisoners in for court. There was little or no hope of them attending on their own.

'You're down at Camp Leichhardt, you said?' Chris asked.

'Yeah, they're quite a bunch. Cross between a retirement village and the Wild West.'

Chris had a bit of a chuckle at that. 'They don't cause me any grief, that's the main thing. From what I've heard they've even got their own laws – think they're a friggin' town or something.'

'They're full of ideas, that's for sure. How are things around here?'

'I've never seen the community so bad. Plenty of alcohol around and even some crystal meth. Domestic violence. One death. Had the coroner out two days ago.'

I couldn't think of anything worth saying, so I just waited until he was ready to go on.

'So, what brings you in here?' he asked. 'You should be out on the river.'

'Had to get a few things at the Bar. Thought I'd come out and say g'day. Besides, I wondered if you might be able to help me with something.'

'Yeah? What with?'

I dug in my pocket and pulled out the black plastic object I had found near the makeshift dock on the lagoon bank. 'You got any idea what this is?'

Chris took it in his hand and turned it over, studying it minutely. 'Where'd you find it?'

'Down the Roper.'

'Yeah, looks like some kind of fishing reel tool. Some of them come supplied for changing spools and that. Must have got dropped.'

'That makes sense.' Strangely, I was a little disappointed. I took the thing back and returned it to my pocket.

Chris cocked an eye at me. 'Can I ask why you

want to know?'

I shrugged. Suggesting that I had misgivings about goings-on at Camp Leichhardt seemed, at this distance, quite ridiculous. A few thugs and one rich old bastard didn't like me being there. They might be up to something. Big deal. What was it? What the hell *could* you get up to out there?

'Nothing really,' I said. 'I'm not exactly Mr Popularity in the camp. One or two of the residents seem like they've got something to hide. I wondered if you'd mind me running a check on them. See if they've got form.'

'Course not.'

Chris handed the baby to his wife, who placed a hand in each armpit and lifted. I stared at the five-month old face, pink toothless mouth cracked into a wide grin, and felt a twinge of ... well, something. That maybe I should be living in some outpost in an official police residence full of nappies and infant formula.

'Come on,' Chris said. 'Follow me and we'll sort this out for you.'

Sitting in front of the computer, cuppa in hand, Chris offered me a few dirty jokes that had already done the rounds in Katherine. Had probably started there. I laughed as if I'd never heard each corny punch line before and watched the screen evolve into the program known generically as LEAP, the Law Enforcement Assistance Program. This was our outdated criminal history and crime reporting database.

'Give us a name,' Chris asked.

'Yates, Terry. Probably Terrence. Heard of him?'

Chris shook his head, lips together so a bristled dimple formed in his chin. 'Nah. Not that I can recall, anyway.' He stopped talking and rattled away with his fingers, waiting while the satellite dish on the roof did its thing and pulsed the request across a thousand kilometres of wilderness.

The mug shot came up, along with an arrest history. We were both quiet, reading through the list, starting with the most recent: using an offensive weapon with intent to intimidate, and going back through DUI, assault, motor vehicle theft. He had done hard time in Berrimah, and there was an alert to some Queensland offences.

'Nice bloke,' Chris said.

'Looks like it. Can you print that off for me?'

'Sure.' I stared at Terry Yates's mug shot while I waited. Pinched lips. Angry eyes. At war with the world. The printer whirred to life and started gobbling paper.

'I'd like to check his brother now. Everyone calls him Wallaby but that won't be his real name. Quieter type. Probably not quite so much trouble.'

Chris jabbed at the screen. 'Here, it says that Terry has a brother called John. That must be him.

Let's run the name and see what we get.'

I was right. John, aka Wallaby Yates had a history, but without the assaults. Robbery with menaces. Nothing for two years. Without me asking, Chris hit the print button and out rolled the paper again.

'Okay, now how about a bloke called Ian Henderson.'

Chris typed away, then hit enter. I craned forward. This was the one I really wanted, and I felt a guilty heat in my face at the reason why. I wanted him to have form a mile long, I wanted it to be even easier to hate the bastard. Maybe even get rid of him. Lock him up.

'Two matches.'

I studied the search result. Both the hits were men too young to be him. 'Nah, unlikely to have done anything here. Try national.'

This was a separate database, and necessitated waiting while the machine ground its way through the connection. We drank tea and chatted while we waited.

The computer found eleven matches, and my friend from the camp was the third we looked at. The mug shot was not recent, but it was him. The file was extensive for a man who had never been inside, despite several arrests and 'suspected complicity' in a number of cases ranging from bribery of police officials to extortion. The word murder jumped off the screen at me. In 1997 he had been questioned in connection with a killing funded by notorious Melbourne gangland figure Mark Moran.

'Straight off Underbelly,' Chris joked, but we were both absorbed.

In 2009 he was arrested for the possession of fifty thousand dollars in cash. His lawyer successfully argued that Hendo had found this windfall on his morning walk. He lost the cash, but walked without seeing a gaol cell.

I stopped reading while Chris again printed up the dossier, leaning back and draining my mug to the dregs.

'You've got some interesting company down there,' he said.

'Seems that way.'

'Are you in danger? You haven't been threatened, have you?'

I shrugged. 'Kind of. There's a lot of hot air floating around. Don't know that I'm too worried yet. More curious as to what the hell's going on.'

'Don't take any risks. Call me straight away if anything happens. Anything. Got it?'

His concern was touching. 'Yeah, I got it. And thanks.'

There was a clang from out towards the road and we both looked up to see a young woman of eighteen or nineteen, baby in her arms, closing the gate and walking up the path towards the station. Her skin was that shiny ebony of the Roper people, the handsome bone structure, high cheekbones, dressed in a pink flowery dress that might have been fashionable in nineteen-twenties Melbourne. Community stores buy such things by the pallet, along with frozen white bread and tins of braised steak and onions.

Chris grunted, 'Ellen. She's a good stick. Often comes to tell me when something's happening.'

She came through the door, shooing the dogs and flies that followed her back through the screen before closing it behind her. Coming up to the counter she looked directly at neither of us, keeping her eyes averted at twenty or thirty degrees.

'Hello Ellen.'

'Hello.'

I could smell the wood smoke and sweat smell of her, not unpleasant when you are used to it. Just different.

'What's happening?'

The baby lay back, arching his spine and crying out. Ellen gentled him with a hand on the back of his head.

The lingua franca at Gajiyuma, along with most Top End communities, is Kriol, a broken English spattered with language from local dialects. Often, English words are pronounced in a way that suits Indigenous consonants, and spelled accordingly.

Old man is marluga. Animal becomes enimul. Numbers start off with: wan, tu, dri. Feller becomes bala. Clever becomes kleba. The Kriol bible, a translation that has been in print for as long as I can remember, calls the three wise men, dri bala klebabala. To have a swim is to bogey. To fight is to fait or have an agyumen. The act of sexual intercourse is, fittingly, called ruding, among other things.

In print, Kriol can sound patronising, but that is a problem for the cross-cultural reader, not the speaker. Kriol is a multifaceted, dynamic language that serves as a bridge between vastly different tongues.

'Big Billy an' Long Joe fait long taim down ribber bank. Joe bleed sleepin' long taim.' Ellen fired the sentence out at speed, making me work to understand the meaning.

'He's hurt bad?'

Ellen nodded.

'Whereabouts?'

'Horse Creek, you know, dat junction d'ere?'

'Yeah. I know it.'

Chris lifted his gun belt from the counter and buckled it on, before picking up the phone and dialling a number. This, it transpired, was the local health clinic. He wanted someone to meet us down there. 'You want to tag along?' he asked me. 'Big Billy can be hard to handle when he's full of grog.'

It would be churlish of me not to help now that I was there. 'Of course I will.'

Chapter Ten

THE OLDER I GET the more I value the truth, and the less I tolerate bullshit. Pretending things don't happen will not make them stop.

The cop 4WD – a Hilux with blue checkered police paint job and a cage, was out in the yard. As Chris and I drove off, I watched Ellen walking away, her face inscrutable.

The community scrolled past me as Chris did his best to climb through the gears despite obstacles such as dogs, kids on bikes, more dogs and rubbish that may or may not be hazardous to a vehicle tyre. A couple of Community Association utes were out and about, collecting bins, delivering firewood. People scarcely looked up from their card games as we passed – big circles under the shade trees, the endless games of cunce and five-card, cash and promises changing hands constantly.

Most of the players were locals but there were

also travelling card 'sharps' who moved between communities fleecing the less skilled inhabitants – a little less commonly since the Intervention reduced the amount of cash in circulation. Even so, the pros could afford the price of air taxis, landing in the right places at the right times – coinciding with welfare and mining royalty payments.

The main part of the community ended, and we drove a maze of tracks down from the bottom of the hill towards the river. The scattered rubbish thinned as we moved further away, but even so, the amount was extraordinary. Burned out cars, discarded nappies, food tins and increasingly, alcohol containers despite us still being within the prohibited area.

The river neared. I could smell it, and then we were above the bank, looking down into a wide flood zone, dense with paperbarks. This was the same waterway, the same Roper River as I had fished for the last few days, but upstream. Still tidal at this point, full freshwater took over at the Bar, where I had done my shopping earlier. Chris committed the Hilux to a steep decline, shifting into low gear and letting the engine do the braking, then accelerating onto the flat, wrangling the wheel to the left and following a track between grey-barked casuarinas, slowing as the first people came into view.

We got out, hearing the shouts, striding fast

along the sand until we saw the man who must surely be Big Billy. His shirt was off, showing a chest raked with ritual scars. He was tall; heavily built, ranting and raving. At his feet lay the prone body of a man. I felt the old anger, yet a sickly resignation. This was the shit I had come out bush to escape.

A drunken woman stood at a safe distance, haranguing, swinging her arms and shaking her head so curly long hair half covered her face. 'You fucking arsehole. You gwei. Leave him alone. Fuck you…' The rant went on and on. A melodious chant and a terrible curse.

Billy, turning to see us walking towards him, ignored her. Instead, he curled one fist into a ball and shook it at us. Even from that distance I saw the bloodshot eyes, the shaking tremens of his limbs. I had seen it before. I knew all about grog. You get that glow in your head and nothing else matters. Only the glow, the chemical glow. No one can stop you. No one can tell you anything.

This man, however, was long past the glow, and into the sick downhill slide, when grog turns on its host organism and does its best to destroy it.

When a human being drinks alcohol for two or three days and nights without stopping – no sleep, no food, just grog – things change. Irrationality, violent mood swings, feelings of persecution or, sometimes, invincibility take hold. Billy was deep in that state, protecting the fallen body of the man he had injured like some kind of predator. Chris stopped, and I stopped with him, watching.

'The one on the ground is still alive,' I said. 'I just saw him move, but looks like a nasty head wound.'

'Yeah.'

I understood Chris's hesitation at moving any closer. People in Billy's state took some stopping. They often hardly felt pain in the conventional sense. 'Is he a local man?' I asked.

'Yeah, but I haven't seen him around for six or eight weeks. Normally a mild kinda bloke, until he gets a gutful of grog. Worked for the Community Association on and off for a couple of years.'

'How do you want to do this?'

'I'll try and talk to him first, but it's like reasoning with a zombie when a bloke gets like this. Stay back a bit if you don't mind. Come in if I need help.'

I did as I was told, remaining still while Chris walked another few paces through the trees. Billy half crouched, watching the cop's approach with slitted eyes.

'Hey, Billy,' Chris called. 'What you done to old Joe there?'

Billy stood tall again and stamped like a bull. 'I hurt him fucking good, you know. Hit him good with a stick.'

'How about you come back to camp with us now?

Have some tucker. I'll cook you up some meat and spuds. Alright?'

While Chris was talking another vehicle pulled up. A white troop carrier with the local health clinic's logo on the side. An Indigenous male and European female got out and walked up. The woman was about twenty-three or four, freckled, with bloodless lips. Her mate hung back, watching.

'Hi, I'm Shona, the community nurse here. Where is the victim?'

I pointed. 'Still out there, unfortunately. You'll have to wait a minute.' I turned my attention back to Chris, who was advancing on Billy.

'I haven't seen you here before,' the nurse said.

'No, I'm a cop up in Katherine, here on holidays.'

A note of disbelief crept into her voice. 'You come here? For holidays? You've got to be kidding.'

'No, not here, downriver.' I turned away. She was starting to annoy me.

Chris took another step and Billy reacted at last. Screaming with rage he brought one foot down hard on the prone man's chest. Ribs broke with an audible crackle. Again the foot came down. Chris had no choice but to go in and I went after him.

Like most good cops in this kind of situation, Chris didn't draw his firearm, instead using speed and footwork to step through flailing limbs and knock the drunk man flying with open palms. I arrived in time to grab Big Billy's arm and twist it up behind his back, a restraining hold that gave Chris time to get cuffs on his wrists.

Billy's victim, I saw, was bleeding from a cut just below the hairline. The nurse and her assistant were already beside him, opening a medic's kit the size of a suitcase.

Even as we dragged Billy to his feet, he was still trying to fight, and it took both of us to get him back to the Hilux and into the cage. We closed the doors, and he hammered on them like a caged buffalo.

'What are you gonna charge him with?' I asked.

'I'll tell you in a second.' Chris walked back to the nurse. 'How bad is Joe?'

'Pretty bad. Probably a skull fracture, maybe a punctured lung.'

Chris turned back to me. 'Attempted murder, wouldn't you think?'

'Yeah, fair enough.'

Yet, there was a gravity in that word murder. And I was thinking, not for the first time, what a prick of a world it was when a man would get pissed off his brain and wake up, sober, in a prison cell, with the word murder on the charge sheet.

I half expected to get back to Camp Leichhardt to find my tent burned down and the boat holed, but nothing had been touched. I unloaded my newly filled water containers, courtesy of a tap at the Gajiyuma Police Station, and made a cup of tea. Chook came over to have a look at my barra fillets, now packed in freezer bags in the Engel fridge.

He stood there in his thongs, blue singlet, and ancient cotton shorts. 'Where'd you find 'em?'

I smiled. 'Can't give away all my secrets, can I?'

'Bastard,' he repeated. 'Want to come over and use the barbie?'

'Might just have a quiet one, if you don't mind.' I ran a hand over my forehead. All the shit, everything I had been trying to get away from, had built up inside me again. I needed silence, just the birds and the crackling fire, and a good morning on the river.

'No worries, but if you feel like company after tea just wander over.'

'Sure, thanks.'

It was almost a relief when he had gone, and I set about the mechanical business of cooking. Dropping the fillets into a hot pan, dusting it with butter, salt, pepper and a squeeze of lemon. That's all a fresh fillet needs. I can vouch for it, having tried fish a thousand other ways. The important thing is to bring it out moist – just cooked, the meat breaking into natural sections and turning translucent, pearly white.

I had just finished eating and was into the cleaning up, washing my few dishes in a plastic tub, when I heard a vehicle, driving at a sedate speed across the track. It was the Yates's old Nissan Patrol, one of the front wheels out of alignment, wobbling like a drunk. I placed the last item face down on the table, before drying my hand on a tea towel.

Stuff them. Their timing was, from their point of view, perfect. Sick to the stomach at what I had seen, confrontation was the last thing I needed. Vehicle doors slammed, and three men entered the fringes of light cast by my hissing gas lantern.

Terry and Wallaby Yates. Ian Henderson. All my fans in one visit, swaggering like the film stars they imagined themselves to be. I waited, arms crossed in front of my chest, trying to figure out some kind of tactic. Once upon a time it would have been easy – fight them. Years ago I had liked fighting, and was good at it. Yeah, even three of them. Taking out Hendo would be a good first move, then concentrate on the other two.

That was the old me. Now the best idea I could come up with was to let one of them hit me and charge him with assault. Take the punch. Drive the offender out to Gajiyuma and chuck him in the cells. Even this was fantasy. The other two wouldn't let me get away with that.

They came closer, stopping a metre or two away. I was braced for a king hit when Hendo stuck his hand out. 'We came over to say sorry. I personally wanted to tell you that I was wrong to say what I said to you, and rude.'

It was my turn to ignore an offered hand. I don't shake hands with verified criminals. Don't believe a word they say either. I switched my gaze to Terry Yates. 'I suppose you're sorry too?'

His smile never faltered. 'Yeah, real sorry. We shoulda made you feel welcome. Not threatened you and all that shit.' Wallaby Yates was nodding along with his brother.

'We all just like the quiet life,' Hendo said. 'Didn't want someone diggin' into everyone's business. I can see now that you're not like that.'

There didn't seem much point in prolonging the pain. I picked up a tea towel and started drying dishes, talking as I worked. 'Well boys, I'd invite you to sit around for a drink, but as you know, I don't have any beer. You can have a coffee if you like?' I saw Terry glance at Hendo, then the shake of the head. I was relieved. I didn't trust these men any more than I could kick them. Socialising as if we were mates would be too much effort.

'Nah, we'll get going,' Hendo said. 'No hard feelings?'

'No feelings either way,' I said, which was not quite true.

They walked back to the vehicle, climbed in and slammed the doors. Waving as they took off. God only knew why they had to drive the four hundred metres down here when any normal human being would have walked.

When they were gone, my pulse stopped racing and I put the billy on, deep in my thoughts, most of them of a suspicious nature.

Chapter Eleven

GOD HOW I LOVED THAT RIVER, the channels and eddies, the sand bars, the limp pandanus clusters, the bony bream flashing in the sun as they fed in the shallows. Even the big dirty crocs catching the sun. Modern day dinosaurs. Cold-hearted bastards that have my deep respect.

I loved the Roper's tides, even now, on the neaps, with one-point-five solid metres racing in and out over a hundred river kilometres, a surge of water that churned and sped, bringing food and pelagic baitfish, cleaning out the system. Bringing life.

I loved running down into the mouth, wind in my hair and the tide moving faster the closer I got, navigating the channels – dangerous stuff, with hidden rocks ready to rip the skeg off the motor. Whirlpools. Bigger, older, and crankier crocs.

The Stessl sat low in the water, with a twenty litre jerrican of petrol on board for back-up. In the rod holders were two heavier outfits, black stubby Shimano TLD20 reels packed with monofilament. One blue line, one pink, so I could tell the difference when they got tangled – always on the cards when trolling.

I timed the tide right, marking a good low water route on the plotter that would get me back through anything. A south easterly wind was blowing and I hit the first chop as I ran through the mouth, navigating between mud banks and giant dead trees carried down in the last flood and deposited in the shallows.

There were two sizable islands offshore from the river mouth. The closest of these was Maria Island, ten miles to the south. I motored towards it at full throttle, bow thumping lightly. I enjoyed the salt air, the occasional fillip of spray that touched my lips. The best part of a mile shy of the island I saw coral pinnacles on the sounder, rising out of twenty metres to just five or six below the surface. I cut the motor back to neutral and grabbed the closest of the two rods, spooled with ten kilo mono.

I had rigged a metre of single-strand wire at the business end, terminating with a clip. Delving in my tackle box I took out a brand new Halco Laser Pro and clipped it on. Within a minute the lure was fluttering behind the boat while I prepared the other line.

Gulf waters don't get the large, rolling swells of the western and eastern seaboards, but can be challenging. Thousands of square miles of relative shallows mean that the wind has a rapid and disturbing effect on the sea surface, building up a chop that can exceed two metres in height, more in cyclonic conditions.

At the moment, the wind chop was a user-friendly half metre or so, and since I was running beam-to it was relatively comfortable. Both rod tips were soon twitching with the action of the lures. I checked them constantly, along with depth readings from the sounder, making sure I was in no danger of snagging up.

Fishing is a great time to think, and many things passed through my mind as I trolled towards the island. Malea was one of them. Her beauty. The strange marriage to Hendo – a man more than twice her age. A man she did not seem to like or respect.

My reaction to women, over the years, has always been one of instant attraction. If it's going to happen it hits me pretty soon, and this one had struck me like a pick handle to the family jewels. I had almost been married once, to the hard-raised, suntanned daughter of a buffalo catcher from Pine Creek. She had a muscular, lithe body, and wallaby-in-the-headlights green eyes, but she met someone else on a boozy Saturday night in Darwin's Vic Hotel just as I was plucking up the guts to offer her my world. Leanne was her name. I still saw her sometimes, and she always greeted me like a long-lost friend, with her horsewoman's stride and tight blue jeans.

Malea, it seemed to me, was a woman I could stand toe to toe with and be equalled in all ways. Her physical competency both surprised and delighted me. Her intellect was at least as sharp as mine. There were hidden depths and undercurrents I sensed and wanted to explore. I did not want to put a name to what I felt for her but I am old enough to know that sometimes you can't help who you fall in love with.

Her husband was a greater mystery still. Why was he here? What was he doing? I sensed that my only chance at Malea was to unlock the mystery, and I made the decision, at that moment, to make Ian Henderson's business my business. Whether he liked it or not, I would unravel a few threads.

The starboard reel screamed like a banshee, breaking my train of thought. I turned so fast the boat rocked. When a Spanish mackerel runs, he runs at a speed only a wahoo or sailfish can match. Mind-blowing. In this case, however, scarcely had I got the rod out of the holder when the run stopped, and the line went slack. I reeled in, disappointed, but pleased that I could still feel the lure on the end of the line – that it hadn't been bitten off above the wire as is sometimes the case.

The brand-new lure, once I reeled it in all the

way, now sported a series of deep gouges along the paintwork, the calling card of *Scomberomorus commerson*, the narrow barred Spanish mackerel. Somewhat flat, yet happy that my chosen technique had drawn some interest, I dropped the lure back out, set the lever drag and replaced the rod in the holder. Having done so I rummaged in my gear bag and pulled out the sandwiches I'd made in the dark that morning, from tinned meat and thawed white bread purchased at the Roper Store.

Despite the plain fare, I ate hungrily, staring back at where my lines sliced through the water, then to the sounder and the sea surface ahead, watching through my polarised sunnies for shallow water over rock or coral. The island loomed closer now, and I studied it with interest. Apart from an offshore outcrop, towering several metres out of the water, it was flat and low, with shelves of brown rock and the odd sandy cove.

I was thinking that it would be a nice place to spend some time with Malea, if our circumstances were somehow a lot different – a bit of swimming, some snorkelling perhaps, lazing around on the beach, driftwood bonfire, night on the sand ...

I heard the other boat long before I saw it, powering south from the river mouth at speed. I have a good ear for outboards, and recognised the roar of the Yates brothers' old Merc. Before long I could see their punt – almost big enough to classify as a small barge – on a heading seaward of Maria Island. Soon it would pass close to my current position.

Certain that they hadn't yet seen me I grabbed first one outfit and then the other, reeling in the lures, hooking the treble hooks on the ferrules and slipping the rods back into the holders.

Starting the Honda, I was away in a surge of smooth power, heading towards the only protection I could see, that small offshore bommie. Terry and Wallaby Yates had not struck me as fishermen, and I could see another tarp-covered load in the boat. If they were up to something I wanted to know just what.

Moving slowly, keeping my head low, I was confident that they had not yet seen me. I headed behind the protective shard of rock and out of sight, skimming over water only two or three metres deep, and clear enough that I could see kelp beds and jagged coral down below.

A bait school broke the surface, splashing silver and white in the sunlight. I would have laid a bet that the kind of predators I was chasing were nearby – slashing, hacking at the baitfish, balling them up until their only avenue of escape was the surface, and that only temporary. As I watched, a Spanish mackerel, rushing up from the deep, jaws slashing, leapt clear of the water, sleek as a bullet.

Those other predators, the men in the boat I had seen, however, were more pressing, and now, half hidden, I waited for them to appear on the other side of the rocks. I didn't have long to wait. Those old Mercs might be noisy, and suck fuel like there's no tomorrow, but they go like the clappers of hell.

For a minute or two I kept my head down and watched. The boat maintained its original heading past the island. If I followed there was a good chance they would see me.

Torn, I looked at where the bait schools still skittered across the ocean surface. Damn it, I decided. I was a cop, even if I was on holiday. Besides, my Stessl was low to the water, and the Yates brothers had not struck me as the most observant of men.

I reached back, shifted the Honda into gear and accelerated after the punt, but not too fast. Prudence dictated that I remained at a distance of around two nautical miles, pretty much the limit of visibility between two small boats on the ocean.

Following the punt became irrelevant, in any case. As soon as I rounded the island the mast and hull of a large cruising catamaran came into view, and I did not have to be a genius to guess that was where the Yates boys were headed.

Chapter Twelve

I DECIDED THAT it was too risky to get any closer to the catamaran. Even then, a watchful person on the deck of the cat might have had me in view. People doing illegal things were usually interested enough to have a good look around.

A breaking reef a couple of hundred metres to the south gave me the opportunity to loiter without looking suspicious. Changing direction, I motored across, and soon had both lures in the water. Anyone with a pair of binoculars on the cat would see me trolling. Enough of a cover, I hoped, to keep them going about their business.

The thought of binoculars had me delving into the front storage locker, where I kept a pair of Zeiss 3 x 28s, handy for spotting bait schools at a distance, checking out other boats and even picking channels through unfriendly river entrances. Taking off the lens caps I sat the instrument on the seat while I finished trailing my lines out. Then, after checking that I was not likely to run aground on that heading, I lifted the binoculars and scanned out to the Yates brothers' boat, now just reaching the cat, a vessel that was even bigger than it had seemed at first glance, pushing fifty feet at the waterline, and at least half that across the beam.

The Yates boys were standing now, their punt tied up to the big cat's stern. I saw the tarp-wrapped cargo clearly, and a man in the rear of the cat, sunglasses on. Wallaby Yates was busy with his fingers, working at a knot, lifting off the tarp and stowing it on the floor of the craft.

My curiosity reached fever pitch. Whatever was in that boat was valuable, but bulky, worth a lot of time, effort and subterfuge.

The starboard reel, the TLD20, suddenly screamed, line peeling out as if it were tied to a passing ski boat.

'Jesus Christ,' I shouted, almost dropping the binoculars. The cop part of me told me to leave the rod, lose the fish, find out what was under that tarp. The fisherman part of me was already reaching for the rod, scarcely able to lift it from the holder such was the power of that run.

The hallmark of a big mackerel is usually, but not always, the length of that first run. Two hundred metres is common, and a really big one will take upwards of three hundred metres of line from a spool, against a drag pressure that might exceed four kilograms.

Judging from the amount of line remaining in the spool when I first started to pump and wind, this one had taken upwards of two hundred and fifty when he finally turned. I worked him hard, casting anxious glances across at the cat and the small boat scarcely discernible by eye, bobbing around at the stern.

With a hundred metres back on the spool, I was beginning to think that he was not so big after all, and that in a few minutes I would be able to sink the gaff into him and get back to studying the cat. At that point, however, he took off again, just to show me who was boss, taking away most of my gains.

Sweat pouring from my face, I worked like a mad bastard, wishing I was wearing my gimbal belt to get some of the pressure off my kidneys, wishing I had twenty kilo line so I could exert some authority, and wishing I could call a truce with the fish for a moment, pick up the binoculars and see what the hell was going on with the Yates brothers.

Fish, however, don't work like that, and he had other ideas, this time a change in direction, pointing his nose directly towards me and running at thirty or forty miles an hour, leaving me turning the reel like a chef beating cream, trying to collect the slack line and get some pressure back on the hooks that he was trying desperately to throw. Finally, with the fish some fifty metres past me, the line came taut again, and I was relieved to find that I was still hooked up. Trophy sized Spanish don't come along every day, and this one was a horse. His headlong run towards me had worked in my favour; put a heap of line back on the spool without the labour of hauling him in.

A few minutes later I got to see him for the first time, a metre and a half of silver javelin, lit up like only big pelagic fish can be, ten metres out from the boat. I guess this, too, was his first chance to see what was happening, and he didn't like it one bit. Again he ran, but he was tired now, managing a mere thirty metres before I pumped him back.

One final run near the boat and I was pretty sure he was mine. The lure looked solid in the side of his jaw, and I wasn't giving him a chance to get those teeth near the line up above the wire trace. Freeing my crank hand for a second I pulled the gaff from its clips and hung it ready on the gunnel.

Now I really gave it to him, skulldragging him beside the boat where he rolled, and I made no mistake with the gaff, jabbing the point deep into his shoulder, half standing so I had the leverage to drag him on board – twenty-five kilos or more of prime eating fish.

For just a few seconds I admired him, filled with privilege and pride, and just that slight twinge of sadness at plucking such a creature from the sea and taking him home in a box of ice. To me, however, catching and killing the food you eat is much more honest than paying others to do the dirty work for you.

This was primeval – clean. Me against the natural world in all its savagery and beauty. Part and parcel of this was a responsibility to keep his flesh in the best possible condition. I bled him carefully, holding the tail, then slid him into the long, insulated icebox, already prepared with a slurry of ice and seawater for just such a catch.

I washed my hands over the side, and dried them on a towel. Still shaking with strain and excitement I lifted the binoculars and scanned back towards the cat.

'Shit,' I spat. The cargo, whatever it was, had gone. Terry Yates was in the process of untying the punt, and Wallaby already had the motor going. As I watched, the man in sunglasses waved goodbye and they picked up speed, heading back north towards the river mouth.

One of them must have seen me. The big punt almost stopped, then turned, heading across towards me, coming to rest at a distance of ten metres, much too close for my liking.

'What are you doing here?' Terry asked. The fake buddy-buddy crap from the previous night was gone, replaced by the old suspicious sneer.

'Fishing,' I said. 'What are you doing? I didn't even see you.' I opened the esky and half-lifted the mackerel. 'What a beauty, eh?'

Terry Yates's guard dropped. 'Yeah, good one. We've been fishing too. Haven't we, Wallaby?'

'Yeah.'

'Do any good?' I asked.

'Nah. Not a fuckin' thing.'

'Too bad.'

Yates brightened. 'See ya then.'

Even though the engine would have been hot, he had to pull start the Merc half a dozen times before it fired. I shook my head at their stupidity. If I was doing something illegal, I would at least make sure I owned a reliable outboard. As they turned tail and ran towards the river I was in contempt of their arrogance. They must have thought I was stupid. As far as I could see there wasn't a fishing rod on the boat.

It was nice to have enough mackerel fillets to share. In the eating stakes, Spanish is about as good as it gets. In certain areas, ciguatera, toxins that move up the food chain in fish, can be a risk with the big specimens, but I'd never heard of it in this part of the Gulf.

I worked on the tables above the ramp, taking off

the first clean fillet, halving it along the lateral line, cutting out the rib bones, and finally flipping it over and skinning each quarter, using a thumb sized slit in the skin to hold each one as I worked the knife blade through.

Some of the Nomads, returning from the day's fishing, came over for a look. Some carried tubs of their own fish – a couple of mangrove jack, a barra or two. Fork tail catfish for the desperate. A pair of old timers called Roy and Christo produced a Nally tub with half a dozen big brown mud crabs in the bottom, trussed up professionally so the claws didn't take the fingers and toes of their captors.

'Bloody good day,' the older of the two, stump legged old Christo, told me. There was something of southern Europe in his voice. Greece, perhaps. 'These crab,' he said, 'they come out of the mangrove at low tide. We use fresh bait; catfish heads. They come into our trap, and we bring them home for supper. I love this place.'

I gave away a chunk of mackerel to anyone who wanted some, and when Chook and his missus appeared, I invited them over for tea, not being sure they'd accept, but in my book, when someone has you over, you have them back, even if your camp is a damn sight more basic than theirs. They too, it turned out, had trapped a couple of mud crabs, and offered them up for an entrée. I wasn't going to say no.

The crowd thinned, and I was just about done when Malea turned up, strolling down to the ramp as people do in places like this, checking out the catch, trying to get a handle on where the fish were biting.

I took my eyes off the job when I saw her, and in the process almost managed to give myself an accidental nick with my filleting knife. It had been a few days since I'd last seen her, and the memory had started to dim. Now it came back in full force. She was wearing a cotton work shirt and tan shorts. Her hair was again tied loosely into a ponytail. She walked with hands in her pockets, smiling as she wandered up.

'Ooh, a big Spanish. You lucky thing. Where did you get it?'

I smiled back. 'Offshore, along a coral bommie.'

'Well done.'

'Do you want some?'

'Really? Have you kept enough for yourself?'

'Are you kidding?' I waved airily at the pile of fillets. 'Look what's left, for Christ's sake. I won't eat that lot in a month.' I lived alone; taking an Engel full of fillets back to town had no appeal for me.

'Okay then. Yes please.'

I trimmed the blood line off a section and sliced it into two sections, I popped one of these into a freezer bag and handed it to her.

'Thank you very much.'

I gave my knife another touch-up on the steel and trimmed the rest of the fillet, packing it also into bags. Then it was time to clean up. The frame I would grill as soon as I got back to camp, throw it on the fire for a few minutes each side, then pick off the meat – it was the best of the lot, so this I laid in the esky over the bags of fillets. The skin, head, and waste meat I bundled up and took a step towards the river, before pausing and smiling at Malea. 'I'm just gonna chuck this down the ramp into the water.'

'I'll come with you.'

'Great.'

As we walked down we talked about nothing and everything. 'You go out fishing today?' I asked.

'No. I had a lot to do around the camp. Maybe tomorrow or the next day.'

'Fair enough.'

At the bottom of the ramp I walked with care. The tide was dropping, and there was a reasonable expanse of mud to cross before I could chuck the scraps in. I stopped before I did so, scanning out across the water. I knew that Malea, beside me, was doing the same thing.

'There he is,' she said, pointing out at the hump of armoured head just above the water, a dark silhouette against the reflected light of sunset. We watched the croc's head slip beneath the water, united in our appreciation of how lucky we were to be able to stand on the banks of a primordial river, and watch a primordial animal do his thing.

I threw the lumps of skin and bloodline underhand, watching as they splashed into the current. Finally I pitched the fish's head, and there was an immediate swirl. Whether it was our ramp croc or a black tip shark I couldn't be sure, but I liked to think it was the former.

'I love this place,' I said on the way up. Dunno why, but I was just, all of a sudden, wildly happy. You know when, unexpectedly, against the odds, there's a point in your life when all the shit just doesn't matter anymore, it's all in the past, and there's just a blinding joy. I knew it wouldn't last, it never does, but that's how I felt at that precise moment.

By the time we reached my vehicle it was getting dark. We chatted like kids, and I should have been rushing back to camp and getting ready for Chook and Shirley coming over but I just wanted to stand there and talk to that woman forever.

Finally, however, it was she who touched my arm and said, 'I'd better be getting back. Ian doesn't like me to get home after dark.'

'Hop in,' I said stupidly. 'I'll drive you.'

'That,' she said, 'would be a bad idea.'

I watched her walk down the darkened track towards the camp and it was a full minute before I got in the Toyota and started the engine.

Chapter Thirteen

CAMP LEICHHARDT'S ODDEST RESIDENT was the occupant of a white Viscount van, streaked with mould, near the river. I'd seen her once or twice around the place, carrying odd equipment, things like butterfly nets, plastic aquaria, and buckets. As far as I could tell she did not participate in the general social scene of the camp.

I met her that evening after my mackerel trip, walking past on my way to the dunnies while she attempted to manhandle a plastic tub the size of a small bath out of the door of her van.

'You want a hand?' I asked.

'No, I'll be right,' she said, but she was a decade or more older than me and obviously struggling – I couldn't resist helping someone in need of some extra muscle.

The tub, it turned out, was half full of water, and weighed enough to put a knot in my shoulders.

Together we dragged and lifted the thing outside.

'Where do you want it?' I asked, and I have to admit I had a quick look down her shirt as it gaped open, and there was no bra to be seen. I got an eyeful of loose little breasts and tiny pink nipples. I think she caught the direction of my eyes, because she gave me a disapproving glance.

'Just get it away from the van a bit so we don't make mud around the step,' she told me.

Together we shifted the tub ten good paces into the darkness away from the van lights before we upended it, and thirty odd litres of water that smelled like effluent from a duck pond drained into the soil.

I stood back and had a good look at the woman. She was medium height, past forty, with hair that had been dyed blonde some time ago, greying from the roots and falling in ringlets past her shoulder. Her skin was pale, considering the latitude, and she had barely perceptible freckles, like the watermark on an old paper note. Her eyes were her best feature, big and blue, with black lashes that radiated like a Japanese fan.

'Thanks for that,' she said.

'No worries. Can I ask what you're up to?'

'Come in and have a look, if you're interested. What's your name?'

'Ben. Yours?'

'Margaret. Call me Maggie if you like.'

I followed her through the door and inside. The dunny could wait, I was curious.

The interior of the van hummed with equipment. The dinette table was set up with a bifocal microscope, lights and glass slides, cover slips, vials of stain and petri dishes. Beyond that was a curtained off bedroom. Where once might have been a galley, was a row of aquaria on shelves, each labelled and filled with vegetation, water and sand. Some had more water than others. My curiosity was aroused. What the hell was in them? I moved up close to look.

I saw small brown frogs with a dark stripe parallel to the body, extending all the way along to the eyes. The kind of frog I had used for bait many times. My eyes moved along to other tanks – part way full of pond water with strings of green algae and fat healthy tadpoles.

I turned to Maggie. 'I take it you don't just do this for the fun of it?'

'No, I'm a researcher with CDU up in Darwin. I'm writing a paper called, 'The Spatial ecology and reproductive capacity of *Litoria wotjumulensis*.'

'I take it that *Litoria* whatsit is these frogs here?'

'That's correct.'

'And you're writing about reproduction.'

'Yes.'

I grinned at her, 'So it's all about rooting, then. Frogs rooting each other.'

She rolled her eyes. 'You really are typical, aren't you?'

'Typical of what?'

'Of blokes, generally. You think you're so funny.'

'Can't help it, sorry.'

She bent down, placed a clear PVC aquarium tube in her mouth and sucked until she got the siphon happening from one of the tanks, a stream of water now emptying into the tub.

She looked at me. 'Off you go now, I've got work to do.'

'Bye then. Yell out if you ever need a hand.'

'I'll be sure to.'

'If I see any of those frogs do you want me to grab them for you?'

'No thanks, I can catch my own.'

'Night is best,' I went on.

'I think I know that, now go on, get out of here.'

Continuing my sociable amble, when I finally got to the dunnies I met an old bloke called Konrad Joseph, just as he was closing the corrugated iron door.

Konrad was tall and thin, with a European accent, as distrustful of authority as any man I have met. Konrad lived by himself, in an antique Globe caravan that looked like it had sat on the spot for several seasons, been abandoned each wet and made habitable again in May when he steered his rusty old XD Falcon north. The only decoration on that renovator's delight was a full-sized Aussie flag up a bush pole.

A tinnie sat on a hand trailer beside the van, a near new fifteen horsepower Yamaha outboard bolted to the transom, looking out of place amongst the relics. Typical fisherman. Got his priorities right. Gotta have a good donk and a boat that doesn't leak. Everything else can be tolerated.

'I like it here,' he said. 'In Melbourne, where I live, a man cannot fart without a permit. You register this, you sign that. You follow council bylaws or you are fucking prosecuted. That is no way to live.'

I nodded gravely. This was a common complaint amongst the Nomads. They had grown up in a more carefree era and seen a half century of bureaucrats regulate life until every little thing was subject to a rule or regulation. That was why they loved it here – but wasn't it strange how soon they had a man calling himself the mayor, and there was a rule about raising dust?

'My daughter tells me that I am cranky old bastard and maybe I am, but I like to come up here and get away from all the bullshit. I like to catch fish too. Fish in the Yarra are all too small and taste like shit. Would you like to see a photo of my daughter?'

'Yeah, why not?'

Konrad switched on his head torch, fossicked through his baggy old trousers and produced a black leather wallet, opening it wide to the display pocket, revealing a matchbox sized shot of a brunette with the face and build of a champion woodcutter.

'Beautiful,' I said.

He smiled happily and put it away. 'Of course she is beautiful. My wife, Anna, was also very beautiful but she died, of the cancer, six- and one-half years ago.'

'That's a shame. I'm sorry to hear it.'

'A shame? Yes. Bad shame. Now I live alone, and I come up here so I can breathe real air and feel like a man with balls again.' He paused reflectively. 'You are a good person, Ben Mulligan. I like you. You want to play cards with me and my friends?'

'Maybe. What's the game?'

'Five hundred. We play at Col Alexander's van. Seven-thirty every night.'

'I'll see how I go.'

'It does not have to be tonight. Any night. We play all the time.'

'Maybe one night, thank you.'

Cooking fish is an art form, and mackerel is my preferred canvas. The meat takes just about any flavour, and cooks firm and white.

Tonight, on top of the world, the ghosts of the

past locked firmly in a padlocked trunk in the back of my mind, with Chook and Shirley sitting by the fire in deckchairs they had carried across themselves, I was inspired to great things, sizzling the fillets in the pan while I prepared a lemon butter sauce in the old cast iron saucepan that had been in the family for so long that the hardwood handle was charred and impregnated with grease and oil. The recipe itself is a ripper, one I pinched off an old girlfriend years earlier. Butter, a juiced lemon and a tablespoon of mustard, poured over the cooked fillets and sprinkled with black pepper.

Once, while Shirley walked back across to their camp for some garlic, Chook reached into the esky sitting within arm's reach, removed a stubby, opened it, then turned to watch her go. I followed his gaze to her dumpy rear end, filling out the faded pink tracksuit pants like twin globes of jelly.

'I'll tell you something, son,' he said to me, in the tone of a master dispensing wisdom to his apprentice, 'when women get older they don't look so good naked any more, but shit, they still feel good.' He said it so sincerely that I couldn't help but believe him.

'I'm sure you're right.'

Chook extended both hands, curling his fingers upwards. 'There's nothing like a big wobbly arse, something you can really get a grip on.'

I laughed then, looking at him with growing fondness.

Chook Fowler was a man with a highly developed sense of humour, and an interesting way of seeing the world. He had, he told me that night, grown up with the union movement in Melbourne. His old man had waved the flag for the Painters and Dockers in their heyday, and he had himself been a shop steward for the Amalgamated Metal Workers Union, formed from a ragtag of boilermakers', blacksmiths' and shipwrights' unions in 1973.

'I'm a union man, yeah, voted Labor all me life, until the day I die.' He smiled and took Shirley's hand when she returned, settling that celebrated rump back into her chair. 'We met up on Election Day, 1972, when Gough Whitlam rolled Billy McMahon. I was scrutineering in Carlton and she was working on the booth, looking up names. Weren't you, darl?'

Shirley nodded, squeezing his hand, and I don't think I ever saw her smile so broadly as she did just then, reminiscing about the day they met. 'Chook was so handsome, Ben. You should've seen him. Such broad shoulders. He came up to me when it was all over for the day, nervous as anything and he said: "G'day, me name's Chook."'

Chook's eyes flew open, leaning forward and laughing. 'That's really what I said.'

Shirley sat up, mimicking the rigid way he held

his chest. "G'day, me name's Chook. You wanna get a pie or somefin'?"'

I laughed fit to bust, but Shirley hadn't finished. Her eyes were astral-deep. Old as quasars. 'Seriously, he was a striking young bloke, strong as a bull, fair knocked me off my feet.' She giggled and flopped one arm around his neck.

Chook held up both hands. 'I was strong because from the day I turned fifteen I worked for a living. Worked with my own two hands and never asked a favour from anybody.' He pointed out at the caravans in the night. 'Not like some of them bastards. Got everything for nothing. Parasites living off the blood of the workers who made this country great. Playin' the stock market like it's a game of Monopoly. Buying houses all over the place and interferin' with people's lives and spending every cent they get on TVs and cars and forty-foot fucken caravans.'

We ate the crabs first, fingers running with juices, using a hammer on a stump to crack the claws. Then came the mackerel. Served with hot spuds done in foil, it was, I had to admit, mouth-watering fare, and know I impressed Shirley, because she made me write out the recipe. Afterwards, we sat together, drinking coffee. Well, apart from Chook, who clung to his VB stubbie. They told me about their kids, grown up and successful. The bush. The state of the country.

Anything.

Once, when Chook rose to piss behind a nearby tree he passed a shelf I had rigged on a tree trunk, and as he went by he picked up something and examined it in his hand. I looked across, seeing that it was the plastic tool I had found by the makeshift jetty in Malea's secret lagoon.

'Apparently that's some kind of fishing reel spanner,' I said. 'Found it downriver.'

Chook scoffed, still holding the thing in his hand. 'No it's not.'

I sat up, interested. 'No? What is it then?'

'One of them little tools you use for installing drippers and sprinkler hoses in the garden – micro irrigation fittings.' He walked across and held it out. 'See the pointy bit, that's what you use to push a hole into the hose. Then you use the spanner end to tighten up the spray fittin'.'

'Are you sure?'

'Course I am. Used one meself.'

Their fat little dog wobbled across to join us, and Shirl lifted him into her lap, crooning and playing with his pointy little ears. His name was Gordon, or Murray or something – all the Nomads liked to give their little dogs human names. 'Chook would know,' Shirley said. 'When we're at home he's always in the garden, or in the shed. Sometimes I can't find him for the life of me, even at dinner time.'

Chook grunted, 'Bloody strange thing to find on a riverbank.'

I nodded, and stared down into my coffee mug.

Chapter Fourteen

GETTING ON THE RIVER EARLY was becoming a habit. Up in the dark, billy on, fill the plunger, then toast smeared with butter and vegemite or jam. Make some lunch, fill a water bottle, then into the Toyota, warming it up against the morning chill then down to the ramp. The last few days I had been first on the water. Most of the Nomads preferred to sleep in a bit.

One morning, the eastern sky glowing with the coming dawn, I looked up from my breakfast coffee to see a tall, lanky bloke walking down the track towards my camp. As he neared I recognised my visitor as the owner of a small Jayco van. A man known universally, it seemed, as the Trout.

The Trout was a strange character, standing maybe six and a half feet tall. His wife was a short-arse, barely five feet, yet there was something about her that suggested she'd been a looker in her day.

'Do you know why they call him the Trout?'

Chook had asked me once, grinning cheekily.

'No, why?'

'Well, he comes from the Snowy Mountains. Place called Talbingo. Used to work for Telstra up there. Apparently he's got a wanger the exact same length as a legal size rainbow trout. So they call him the Trout.'

'Wanger?'

'You know, his old fella.'

'Oh,' I said, interested enough to enquire, since I was familiar only in vague terms with that species of fish, what the legal size might be.

'Twenty-five centimetres. Ten inches,' Chook informed me.

A few moments passed while I digested this information.

'It's true, you know,' Chook hastened to add. 'I seen it meself. One day he was having a piss down at the ramp. You should've seen the size of the thing. Half way down his fucken leg, would you believe it?'

'I believe it,' I said gravely, and while that intelligence was of some interest, it did not help to explain why the owner of this miracle was ambling up the track towards me before the dew had stopped falling. I was anxious to get fishing, and was tired, maybe a little irritated.

The Trout approached the campsite in a roundabout way, like a dog looking for a good spot to have a piss, sniffing here and there before making a decision, stuffing his hands in his pockets and walking up to the fire.

'G'day,' he said.

'Hi. You're up early.'

The Trout made a show of pulling his hands out and warming them at the fire. Still in that pose, he twisted his head to nod at my boat, all decked out ready to go. 'You goin' out?'

I grinned. 'Won't catch anything staying here.'

More silence while the Trout continued to toast his hands, brow furrowed as if deep in thought.

The wait got the better of me. 'Can I help you with something?'

The Trout nodded at last, then reached down between his legs to adjust a python-like appendage that was just visible down the front of his track suit pants. I felt like telling him that a bloke with that calibre of equipment really needed to kit himself up with underwear when he finally decided to spill the beans.

With an angry twist of his lips he jabbed a thumb back towards Hendo's giant caravan. 'Those pricks over there,' he said, 'they're up to something.'

'Yeah, what?'

The Trout shrugged. 'Fuck knows. Bad shit.'

'What makes you say that?'

He kicked at the dust with one boot, and tears

welled up in the craggy old face. 'Hendo poisoned my dog. Well, the missus's dog really. Poor little bastard.'

'Shit. That's a prick of a thing to do. Why would he do that?'

'Horrie – that was his name, went over there all the time. Took a shine to Hendo's missus and I had to keep going over, getting him back. Last night he started shitting slimy green shit and then he died.'

I didn't know what to say. 'You sure Hendo did it?'

'I can't prove it or nothing, but I know he did. I wouldn't have worried you, but my missus wanted me to come over and tell you. We haven't had a wink of sleep. She bloody cried all night. Had that dog for nine years.'

'What do you want me to do?'

'Dunno. There's nothing you can do, I guess.'

'Not really. Just keep my eye on them.'

'They must be up to something ... they didn't want my little dog going around there. Not only that but I've heard stuff – nothing concrete, but everyone knows there's something going on.'

'Tell your wife I'm sorry, and if I can find out anything I will.'

'Yeah, thanks.' He started to turn, then, as an afterthought he said, 'I heard you don't drink.'

I rolled my eyes. 'I guess a man's got to be famous for something.'

'I don't drink either. Haven't had a swig for thirty odd years.'

'Well done.'

I waited for him to tell me why, there always had to be a reason. People don't just stop drinking without good cause. I'd heard plenty of variations.

'Some people just shouldn't drink,' he said.

I tipped the dregs of my coffee into the coals, walked to the half-full wash basin and rinsed out my mug. 'I think you're right there.'

'I was an arsehole,' he said, 'on the grog. Lorna put up with it for seven or eight years. I turned into a mean bastard when I was drunk. I hit her once, you know, and that was it.' He coughed into his hands. 'I woke up the next morning and she didn't say anything, just had this fat lip and blood on her nightie. Nearly went out to the shed and put a bullet in my brain that day, and I needed another drink so badly ...'

I was drying my coffee mug and my hand started to rattle and shake so bad I dropped it on the ground. I turned on him. 'I'm sorry about your dog, but I don't really need your life story, right?'

The hurt was plain on his face, but he made no move to leave.

I covered my eyes with the palm of my hand. 'I'm sorry, look, I didn't mean it. I just get sick of people asking why I stopped drinking.'

'Nah, my fault. I had no cause to go running off at

the mouth.'

I held out my hand. 'Sorry, mate.'

'Yeah, sure, I understand. Some people don't like to talk about it.'

I looked at him strangely. 'I'll keep an eye on Hendo and the others. If I think I can prove anything I'll let you know.'

We shook again, then he ambled away, a sad old man. When I finally loaded up the rods and headed down towards the ramp, that old familiar melancholy had a firm grip on my psyche.

I fished half-heartedly a mile downstream for three or four hours. I was hoping Malea would show up, but she didn't.

I went back to camp early in the day and did some chores – getting the chainsaw out and cutting a shitload of firewood – enough to drop off a pile at Chook's camp and the same amount for Konrad. Thanks to my old man I'm good at bush work – all kinds of things – sharpening tools, swinging an axe, and basic bush mechanics. Dad was big on the idea that once a man was past his prime his main role was to impart the wisdom of his years to those still finding their feet in the world.

On Saturday afternoons he would take me down to the shed and show me how to change a hacksaw blade, how to hone a knife on a stone spattered with sunflower oil so that the blade shaved hair from his arm. He took me out bush and showed me how to shoot, how to butcher a steer. Not only that, but he talked to me constantly, instructed me on everything from the need for compromise in relationships to handling work colleagues. Dad wasn't always right, but mostly he was, and the rest of the time he was close enough.

That evening I prevailed on Chook to partner me at the Five Hundred game Konrad invited me to attend. This was an education. All the players were dyed-in-the-wool Grey Nomads, and I had the opportunity to study them; try to understand what made them tick.

They were mostly practical types: farmers, tradies or blue-collar professionals from small towns and the outer suburbs of major cities. The paraphernalia they packed and brought North never failed to surprise me. More than one of the Camp Leichhardt crowd had lawnmowers to keep their patch of dust weed free. Satellite dishes were essential, as were chainsaws, boats, gas hot water heaters, inverters, iPads, portaloos, separate toilet tents and wee buckets.

Gearing up was understandable. These people come here to live, not just visit. There was even a polite snobbery about which section of the camp you inhabited.

Being too close to the dunnies was a bad thing. That's where you found the real clapped out vans. There was a row, along the river bank, that qualified as snob hill, dominated by Hendo's colossal extravagance, the Wildcat. Some of the others would have pushed into that price range, but were not quite so spanking new as his.

The men around the table, and they were all men, were not what I would call 'good' card players, and all seemed to have hit the grog before their arrival at the game, and were still clutching stubby bottles. One or two sported half empty wine bladders.

I had attended some drunken, confused card games before but this one took the cake, the combination of age and alcohol producing the seven most careless players I had ever seen. They giggled incessantly, and to make the noise factor worse, other, non-playing spectators turned up to watch, talking and arguing in the kitchenette and annexe.

'I'll go eight spades,' Chook said, and I shook my head slowly, as if to say, *Don't do it, you stupid old bastard*. You'd think he would have known ... when I had just gone seven diamonds. He gave me a guilty shrug as if to say, *It's only a game*. Well, that was true, but to me the fun of playing games was trying to win them. Chook went on to lead the nine of clubs and I felt like banging my head on the table. If he had been partnering my old man he would have got a kick in the shins for that one.

'What's trumps again?' someone asked – the first of maybe five-thousand times the question was asked that night.

I heard stories that would curl your hair and sour the milk in your coffee. Some of these old blokes cared not about the bounds of decency. I learned that older people, in general, have a vibrant sex life, but one littered with more problems than rewards. I heard more about KY jelly, haemorrhoids, catheters, Viagra, and testicular deformities than I had in all the previous years of my life.

Two of the hangers-on had a heated argument about the merits of using a load levelling kit on a twin axle van. This kind of discussion was part and parcel of their world. A world centred on equipment. Hayman Reece towbars, adjustable hitches, sensabrake systems, bearing oilers, grease nipples. These old blokes loved it all. Were obsessed by the minutia of the caravanning life. A discussion of tyre choice can while away an evening. Pulling apart, reinstalling and bleeding a hydraulic brake system was a top way to spend an afternoon.

If they weren't talking about gear, they were talking about roads, and routes. The best route through Queensland was a popular argument. Once agreement had been reached on this, they moved onto the best stopover towns, and then the cheapest caravan parks or free rest areas in which to camp. Which parks had clean bathrooms, inexpensive washing machines or cranky owners. Which rest areas might see the local cops move you on at two in the morning because there were 'no camping' signs. Finally, they talked about fishing and boating. Most, but not all, were obsessed with fishing.

The game went on until about nine thirty, when half the players were asleep, or their wives, clad in dressing gowns, carrying dolphin torches or wearing head lamps, came to lead them away. I left with Chook, philosophical now, especially since we had somehow managed to snatch a narrow win, dribbling past five hundred points, the magic number, despite all his efforts to throw it away.

I left him outside his van, babbling something incomprehensible about a practical joke he had once played on an apprentice. Walking away, a light came on and I heard him pissing against a tree while Shirley called him to bed from the door of the van.

Instead of heading for my own camp, however, I walked down towards the river, upstream from the ramp where rocks fringed the water, choosing a spot a respectful distance from the edge. I shone my torch beam out into the water, noting the orange traffic-light eyes of a couple of crocs reflecting back at me.

The rattle of frog calls was a constant background, and the sky a black glossy canvas pinpricked with the stunning light of the stars. The bush is rarely fully dark – only thick, low cloud can make it so.

Switching off the torch I smiled to myself – ticked off my favourite constellations – the scorpion, the crab; all those white man's dreamtime stories that so enriched my childhood camping trips, my old man pointing resolutely upwards, waiting until I 'got' the picture, his breath thick with Johnny Walker. Then he'd tell me the story of Lupus, the wolf, or the seven sisters, the Pleiades, daughters of Atlas, shining like the jewels in a crown, so vividly I could weep at how each took her own life, before being immortalised as stars by Zeus, king of the Gods.

Sitting down on a river stone, I watched the nocturnal activity on the river; flying foxes squabbling in the mangroves on the opposite bank, the plop of a mullet launching itself into the air, before smacking into the surface. Strange how much a part of it I felt, and when I thought back on the Nomads and that crazy maddening card game, I understood that they had a strange relationship with this place.

When you bring a house on wheels into the bush, you have changed location, but the comfort stops the connection. The roof over your head blots out the stars. The electronic chatter of the television, and Facebook on the iPad screen helps to shut the night out. I had heard one of the old girls express the opinion that the insect and bird noises, after dark, were frightening.

Frightening I can live with. The night should be just a bit frightening. There is always that dark thing. The one that growls like a dog and brings the hairs on the back of your neck prickling until they stand like the bristles of a hairbrush. The curlew's cry brings a lot of green bushies undone, as does the hiss of a quoll.

Having spent hundreds if not thousands of nights alone in the bush, I've learned not to think about it too much. I've known for a long time that the thing to be feared most of all is buried deep in the grey folds of the brain.

I sat for a few more minutes, picking over the bones of the night, coming to the realisation that I didn't want to go to my bed alone. That I was jealous of these married couples who laughed and bickered good naturedly like old mates.

Finally, I stood up, brushed off the seat of my shorts, stretched, took a last look around and started back towards camp.

Having reached the flatter ground above the high bank I heard the sound of a distant gunshot, crackling and echoing from far away rock ridges and hills. I stopped walking and heard it again. Five or more kilometres away.

There were plenty of innocent explanations for a gunshot out here. Euthanizing injured livestock. A wild dog caught in a spotlight. Pig hunting. It wasn't my business, or concern, but still it made me nervous.

I unrolled my swag and laid down, heavy lidded but with a heart filled with misgivings. Everything I knew about the world told me that danger was coming, and that I would be in the thick of it.

Chapter Fifteen

'HEY BEN, YOU'D BETTER COME WITH ME,' Chook said, appearing at my camp not long after sunrise. 'Old Konrad's had a punch up with someone and he's copped a hiding.'

I lifted the pan off the gas ring and raised my eyebrows in surprise. Konrad was an argumentative old bastard, but who in hell would want to fight him? 'Who did it?'

'He's not saying.'

After tipping the eggs and bacon onto a plate and covering them with foil, I followed Chook down the track to Konrad's little Globe van. Half a dozen Nomads in pyjamas were talking in groups outside. They stopped as I approached and I nodded politely, walking into the annexe with its food and canvas smells, then into the van itself. Konrad was on the bed, bloodied and moaning, doing his best to swat away Mayor Davis and another old bloke, both trying to clean up the dried blood and get an ice pack onto his face.

Whoever had done the job on him had done it well. The cut under one eye needed stitches, and his nose looked like it was broken.

When I moved closer Davis scowled at me protectively.

'He don't need a cop, just a doctor.'

'Maybe he needs both,' I said. 'Who did this?'

Konrad broke into a rant. Aussie swear words interspersed with a guttural language I didn't understand. German, I guessed.

'He won't tell us,' said Davis. 'So I don't think he's gonna tell you either.'

'Why don't you shut your mouth and get out of the fucking way?'

He harrumphed at me, sidestepping past and out of the van without saying another word.

'Konrad,' I said, 'you know I'm a cop, don't you?'

'Yes.'

'I need you to tell me what happened so I can decide if this has to go further.'

His face screwed up as if trying to control the pain. 'I had a little fight with one of my friends. That is all.'

'After the card game?'

'Yes, after cards.'

'Which friend?'

'I will not say, they are my friend.'

I didn't get it. 'Where did it happen?'

'At the dunnies.'

'What about?'

'Just a silly joke that got out of hand. It was nothing. Leave me alone, please. I am not hurt that bad.'

I squeezed his shoulder affectionately. It was hard to blame him for keeping his mouth shut. This was a small community and dobbing someone in was not going to endear him to whoever did this. 'Call me if you change your mind.'

'I won't change my mind. It was nothing. Forget it. Go fishing.'

At first I started back towards my own camp, but by the time I was almost there I changed my mind and set off at a rapid stride towards the Yates boys' caravan with their vehicle sitting, streaked with dew, beside it. I walked up to the van door and started hammering.

A voice from inside; 'Who is it?'

'Ben Mulligan.'

'Fuck off then.'

'If you don't open this door in five seconds I'm gonna get on the phone. I'll have a warrant so fast your stupid head'll spin.'

Another voice. Terry. Whining. The persecution

complex rising to the top. 'A warrant? What the hell for?'

'How about possession of an unregistered firearm?' A wild guess, but it was enough to get the door open.

The van rocked to a series of footsteps. Wallaby opened the door, wearing nothing but a filthy pair of stubbie shorts, hairy white gut hanging over the waistband. 'What makes you say that?'

'Never mind right now. I want to know what you were doing last night after ten. Someone bashed old Konrad and I can't think of anyone else here who might have done it except for you two.'

'Wasn't us,' Wallaby smirked. 'We was both in bed asleep by nine. Weren't we, Terry?'

The other brother came up from behind. 'That's right, cop. Wasn't us.'

'Can anyone confirm that?'

'Yeah, we were with Hendo until about then, and he walked us back here. Would've seen the lights go out, I can bet on it.'

Yeah, me too, I thought bitterly.

Terry snarled, 'You finished? Mind if we go back to bed?' The hand on the latch exposed the knuckles of his right hand. I saw red smudges where skin had come off. On someone's teeth and bone. He saw me looking too. He saw and didn't care.

'Yeah,' I said. 'Quite finished.'

It took me five seconds to clear Konrad's van of volunteer nurses and well-wishers. When they were gone, I sat on the edge of the bed.

'Why did Terry Yates hit you?' I asked.

Konrad stared at me, shaking his head.

'You have to help me on this. I heard gunshots last night. Did you see something you shouldn't have?'

'No. Leave me alone.'

'Did they threaten you? Did they say that if you said anything they'd come back and finish you off?'

'Nothing. Please.'

Standing, I shook my head slowly. 'You have no idea,' I said, 'how much I hate people like them.' It was true. Bastards who use physical power as a weapon. To intimidate. To hurt. To take things and money that aren't theirs. 'When I pin them, I want you to make a statement. Think about it. You can help me put them away.'

His eyes steadied. He trusted me. 'I will think about it.'

'I'm going to see Davis. He'll take you into Gajiyuma and get the nurse to have a look at you. Don't argue.'

He didn't say a word as I left the van. I found Davis in his annexe, pouring a tin of vile smelling canned food into a pot and heating it on a gas burner.

'Turn that off,' I said. 'You're gonna take Konrad

in and get him stitched up.'

'Am I? Who says?'

'I do.'

'Or what?'

'I'll arrest you for obstruction.'

'Obstruction of what?'

'You don't need to know that yet, just be bloody certain that I will. Got it?'

Davis turned the dial off on the cooker then leaned down to turn off the bottle. Then he picked up his keys from the table. 'I was going to take him in anyway. I don't need you bullying me.'

I patted him on the shoulder. 'Good man. I'll check on him when you get back. Be nice to him or you'll answer to me.'

He muttered something under his breath, but at that point I couldn't really care less what it was.

Most days I had pointed the boat downstream. Today, however, I headed up. For the last hour or so I had weighed and considered the physical evidence like a one-man courtroom. Exhibit A was the sound of gunshots echoing over the valley late at night. Exhibit B was a man with a smacked-up face who was too scared to say a word. Exhibit C was a black tool used for irrigation fittings. Exhibit D was a pair of Roper men running away through the bush and a smooth indentation on the riverbank. Now, thanks to Chook,

I had an idea just what might have left such a mark.

The tide was high, and the deeper water helped me all the way to the first set of rapids, then the second, beyond which the river was still tidal, yet scarcely so at this time of year, when the river levels had dropped, and more particularly on the neaps. After the third cascade, as I entered the long slow pool I had fished just a few days earlier, I tasted the water and it was, for all intents and purposes, fresh, with just the faintest brackish taint.

Scanning ahead, I picked out the place where I had seen the two men. I dropped the revs right back. The Honda was quiet, but not completely silent, and I was not stupid enough to telegraph my arrival. Letting the keel touch the mud bank I clambered out and tied up to a protruding root.

There, with the last ripples from my wake pushing against the bank, I kneeled down and again studied a flattish impression against the mud of the bank. No, it had not been my imagination and no, it was not natural. I looked warily inland, knowing that from here I should proceed with caution.

Walking silently, I followed a clear path through the undergrowth, bare sand in most places, the casuarina trunks tall but not thick, with their dark, scaly bark. One or two brown frogs hopped away from my feet and I thought of crazy Maggie, wondering if I should catch a couple for her.

Fifty metres on, I came up to the hollowed-out remnants of a big old paperbark. In the interior sat a near brand-new Davey fire-fighting pump and a roll of lay-flat irrigation pipe. I sat on my haunches and studied it.

As all good cops know, there is a moment in every investigation when suspicion finds hard cold fact to bed down on. The recognition of the moment was so strong that the goose pimples rose on my forearms. Leading from the pump, further away from the river, was an unbroken line of 32mm black poly pipe. I rose, and followed.

The pipe led me on another hundred metres or more, at which point it reached a chicken wire fence as high as my waist. Whoever erected that barrier had not bothered to install a gate, and I did as they had done, simply climbed over.

On the other side my nostrils filled with the sickly sweet smell of *Cannabis sativa*, Indian Hemp. The plants were growing between native trees, laden heavily with seed heads, attended by hordes of bees.

I stopped dead, mouth open so that my breath whistled in my teeth and dried my lips. I was now in extreme danger. Just by being here, just by knowing, I was a threat to someone. Someone who might already be watching me.

Walking on another few paces I realised that this was a big plantation: hundreds of plants, maybe thousands. There was no point continuing. I turned and walked back the way I had come, as silently as possible, trying not to leave clear prints or sign. Over the chicken wire. So far, so good, but still with the feeling that I was about to get a high-powered bullet between the shoulder blades.

Past the pump, half hidden in its tree, then to the riverbank, footfalls soft on the mat of melaleuca roots, I reached the spot where I had tied the boat – just in time to see it floating away down the pool, spinning lazily into the current.

'Shit,' I shouted, and loped off after it.

One thing I have been able to do since childhood, is tie a knot that will not work its way loose. Someone had been watching. Someone had loosened the knot for me and let the boat go.

Chapter Sixteen

RUNNING THROUGH THE DENSE riverine scrub, I was determined not to let the boat out of my sight. The current was not swift, but the going was hard: a muddy inlet here, a dense thicket there. Leaves whipped across my face as I ran, and I copped more than one low-hanging spider's web along the way.

The Stessl went into an eddy, beginning a long, slow spiral that took it close to the far bank, so that I gained on it easily. It was, however, still separated from me by twenty metres of deep water.

Swimming across to get it was an option, but the presence of saltwater crocs was enough to make me pause for thought, even with a boat and near new outboard at stake.

Whoever let the boat loose might be nearby. They might be armed. In fact, I had never heard of men tending drug crops *not* to be armed. They were as much at risk from rip-off gangs as the police and rarely went about their business without shotguns or rifles. Swimming across with the crocs and the chance of someone shooting at me was too risky to contemplate, so I waited, willing the boat into the fast water. The cascade was only a few hundred metres away now. I hoped I'd be able to clamber out to meet the boat there.

Slowly the Stessl began to drift back into the current. I made an exclamation of relief as I ran after it. A jumble of rocks and boulders blocked my way; both slippery and treacherous. I hopped from one to the next, ankles and knees buckling with the strain. The boat was now into the initial pull of the fast water, spinning once, hurtling for a few metres before coming to an abrupt halt, hitting a protruding stone with a metallic clunk, hovering there for precious seconds.

I moved on downstream before I started across, as the worst possible result would have been for the boat to float down past me before I managed to get into position. As I entered the knee-deep water I was still faced with randomly strewn boulders, but now they were slippery with algae. I blundered forward, feeling my knee strike stone, swearing, looking ahead to where the Stessl had broken free of the obstruction. It was now hurtling down current at a scarcely believable speed.

The angle, however, was wrong. I was ten paces

shy of where I needed to be. Ten paces of slick rock and white water. Wallowing like a water buffalo I lurched across, using every reserve of strength and endurance, flapping with my hands at the water surface like a rower as if to speed my way.

For a moment it looked like the boat would pass me by, but with a last desperate lunge I caught the stern with the fingers of my right hand. The water was shallow enough for me to throw a leg over and settle into the seat, leaning back as the hull spun again, caught and continued before shooting the last section of rapid like a kayaker, jarring on rock and pulsing forward in a manner I'm sure the manufacturer never anticipated.

Unexpectedly, then, the air around me was disrupted in a hammer blow of sound that had me cowering to the deck. Again it came, just as the boat lurched into the calm waters at the end of the cascades. This time something struck the water, and a fountain burst into the air, splattering the boat with spray. I did not have to be a genius to know that someone was shooting at me. Turning, I looked back up to the top of the cascade where two distant and unrecognisable figures were standing. One held a rifle to his shoulder and fired again. This time the bullet passed so close that I swear I felt the wind of it on my cheek.

Keeping low, I reached out, tilted down the

outboard and pulled the starter. Twisting the throttle, I accelerated downstream at speed, leaving the men and their rifle behind.

I had no way of knowing how fast the lines of communication were, or whether there was any link between the illegal gardeners upriver and Hendo's cartel at the camp. Instinct told me that the connection was more like steel cable than cotton thread. That there would be repercussions for my discovery.

The one thing on my mind was to get a message out as fast as possible. Using the ramp, however, might not be a good idea. Instead, I stopped shy of the camp and motored deep under the overhanging branches of a mangrove, where I moored in a small, dark inlet. From there I stepped ashore, negotiated a muddy bank and walked up to the top, ooze squeezing between my toes and clinging to my ankles.

I was upstream of the camp, the first vans perhaps two hundred metres away. Still unsure of what to do, I began to skirt the cleared area, staying under cover of the light woodland, yet moving as fast as the terrain would allow me.

One of the nearest vans was Hendo's big Wildcat, and I crawled towards it, keeping to the longer grass.

Having moved as close as I dared, I waited, lying prone, watching. There was no sign of life until Malea came out of the annexe carrying a basket of washing. This she began to peg on a series of ropes strung between a pair of smooth-barked woollybutt trees.

The sun was high by then, and I slipped the stainless-steel Seiko watch from my wrist, holding it at the correct angle, seeing with satisfaction that it produced a small but intense ray of light that I could direct with some accuracy. I rose to my knees and directed the ray out at Malea, who was half facing me. I watched an expression of annoyance as the dot of light crossed her face, and one hand rose to shield her eyes before she went back to her washing.

Again I aimed the beam at her, and now she put down the shirt she had been about to hang and started to walk towards me. Even as she came I did my best to keep the ray in her eyes.

At the verge of the bush she stopped, and I stood up, beckoning to her before sinking back down out of sight. She hurried now, smiling, slipping down on the earth beside me, touching my arm and giggling.

'What on earth are you doing, Ben?'

'I wish I knew. Where's Hendo?'

'I'm not sure. He had a call on the satellite phone about half an hour ago. After that he went over to the Yates's van and they all went off together. Why?'

I had no idea how much to tell her, wasn't even

sure if I could trust her. Hell. I wanted to, and was pretty sure I could, but sometimes pretty sure wasn't good enough. 'Have you got a mobile phone?'

'Not with me, it's back in the van. Do you want to call someone?'

'Yes. I'd use mine but it's in the Toyota, right over the other side of the camp.'

'I'll go get it. Back in a minute.'

I watched her go, heart in my mouth. All she needed was to get a message to her husband and I was sunk. If that was her plan, however, she must have done it fast, because she stepped into the annexe and reappeared a moment later with something in her hand.

Watching her walk back towards me, I realised the strength of the hunger inside me. It had been a long time since I'd really liked a woman. This one was something special.

Coming back with the phone she squatted on the grass beside me then passed it across. An iPhone. I turned it on, hearing the schmoozy electronic welcome as I did so. The wallpaper was of Malea herself, holding up a threadfin salmon that would have gone five kilos.

Just before I started tapping out the number, I turned to Malea and studied her seriously. 'I found some men doing something illegal this morning. Your husband may or may not be connected with it.'

Her eyes never left mine. 'Ian is a man who makes his own choices.'

The answer thrilled me. This was not the voice of a woman in love. I put the call through, waiting for the signal to bounce off the tower beside the big covered trailers, then away into the ether to some satellite or other, then finally onto the dish atop the Gajiyuma cop station.

The ringing sound came, then Chris's voice at the other end.

'Hello, Gajiyuma Police.'

'Hey, Chris. Ben Mulligan.'

'Hi there, what's up?'

'You busy?'

'Yeah, rough day, a couple of violent domestic disputes. Got six blokes and a woman in the cells now. Gonna need a bloody minibus for the next court session. By the sound of your voice you're about to make it even busier ...'

'Found a dope crop, mate. Big one, professional outfit. A couple of locals were on the scene, but I doubt they dreamed it up all by themselves.'

'Yeah? Where is it?'

'About fifteen klicks north of here by river. Southern bank. Thought you might want to call in some help. Chopper maybe. Soon see if there's any more around.'

'Yeah, could do that. Might be an idea just to get

you to show me first. Keen to have another look?'

I grimaced. 'Not too keen. They were shooting at me, Chris. Wasn't pleasant having bullets whipping around my head.'

'Guns too.' He whistled. 'Still, I'll come down and we'll have a quick poke around. I might be able to suss things out a bit better than the Darwin boys. They're not exactly subtle, are they?'

He had a point. The so-called experts might miss clues and signs that Chris would recognise straight off. 'No they're not, you're right there. Where do you want to meet?'

'There's a track into the area you're talking about. Used to be a small outstation. You know that second jump-up after the old airstrip?'

'Yeah.'

'Just after you come back down onto the plains there's a lay-by. Wait for me there.'

'Sure. When?'

'An hour. That alright?'

'Fine. I'll see you there.' I pressed the end call button, and closed the phone, handing it back to Malea. I said, 'I'll pay for the call later.'

'No, don't worry about it. You think that Ian is growing marijuana?'

I shook my head. 'I think that your husband is way too smart to touch the stuff, but I've got an idea he's involved, somehow.'

Malea paused. 'You know the lagoon where we went fishing.'

How could I ever forget? 'Of course.'

'I didn't really find it myself on Google Earth, you know.'

'No?'

'Ian did. We went there one day, with Terry Yates. They made that dock, and they unloaded something, then loaded something back up. Ian doesn't know I go fishing there.' She paused. 'I'm really sorry I didn't tell you before.'

'That's fine, I understand.' I studied her face. It seemed to me that the almond shaped eyes betrayed more than a trace of guilt. She hadn't exactly lied to me, but she'd held quite a bit back. Still, the guy was her husband. I couldn't find it in my heart to hold it against her. 'The stuff they were unloading,' I asked. 'Was it bulky?'

Malea nodded. 'Very much so, and some of it looked heavy.' She screwed up her eyes. 'There were coils. Big black coils.'

That made sense. 'Irrigation pipe.' The dripper tool now made perfect sense.

Malea shrugged. 'Perhaps. I am not allowed to see anything. Not really. When Ian needs to do something he sends me off fishing, or gets one of the Yates brothers to drive me to Katherine, shopping.' She shuddered. 'I hate them both – Wallaby and

Terry. They give me the creeps.' She gripped my shoulder, not hard, but the touch was electrifying. 'There may be worse to come than just a marijuana crop.'

'What do you mean?'

'I'm not sure so don't press me. I ask Ian no questions. I see nothing. I am the dutiful wife. I fish, I cook. I sleep with him when he asks me to.'

Her eyes had the force of hydraulic clamps on my heart. Was she telling the truth? Her husband and his mates were into some horrible shit. Was she part of it all? I had to know. 'Do you love him?'

'No, Ben, I don't love him. But I can't leave him, either.'

'Why not?'

'Just because, okay? Leave it at that, and let's not talk about it again.'

I made a comb with the fingers of my right hand, and raked it through my hair, finding and removing a dry leaf that I must have picked up from some overhanging branch on the riverbank. I crushed it in my hand, inhaling the strong, astringent scent of it. 'So the Yates boys and Hendo are all out somewhere?'

'Yes, they left about an hour ago.'

'Then there's no point hiding.' I stood up. 'I'd better get going.'

Malea moved her hand from my shoulder to the back of my neck. It was a mixed message that both confused and thrilled me. 'Be careful,' she said softly. 'If someone was shooting at you ...'

'I'll be right. Don't worry about me. It's my job.'

We walked together as far as the Wildcat before I continued on my own. Davis was sitting in a cheap folding chair outside his annexe staring across at me. I wondered how deeply he was involved in whatever the hell was going on around here. I hoped the crappy chair would collapse and leave him sitting on his bony old arse.

Chapter Seventeen

DROPPING THE TRAILER off back at camp, I cruised slowly out towards the main road. I passed two LandCruiser/camper-trailer combos heading in, shiny new tinnies upside down on the racks. These were a different crowd – family travellers living the dream, kids craning forwards from the back seat, fired up with the mystique and excitement of the Territory.

The meeting place was a good twenty minutes away, and I was pleased to see Chris's police Hilux already there. He stepped out, waiting for me as I pulled up, dressed in his khaki shorts and shirt, orange police badge on each shoulder. On his feet he wore black boots and green cotton gaiters. The sight of him gave me confidence. The law did have a presence out here, and Chris was a competent looking bloke.

'Didn't expect to see you again so soon,' he said.

I grinned. 'Neither did I. Didn't expect to stumble on a gunja crop out here, either.'

'It happens. Not often, but sometimes. Just hold on, I'll get a map and see if we can pinpoint the location.'

With the 1:100000 topo map spread out on the bonnet I traced the course of the river up from Camp Leichhardt, checking for landmarks and distances. Finally, I used the tip of a pencil to place a mark lightly beside the snake-like blue wanderings of the river.

'Here,' I said. 'Or close enough.'

Chris took the pencil and traced a line through the air a few millimetres above the paper. 'There's a track through here. We can drive to within about six or seven hundred metres and bush-bash or walk from there.'

'Sounds good. I'll lock up and climb in with you.'

The diesel engine growled at low revs, delivering plenty of torque for the shallow dips and gullies we encountered on the road in. The soil was sandy, and soft pits were the main hazards, most of which Chris deftly avoided. He spent half his waking hours driving on these kinds of surfaces and he was good at it.

Even so, this was the kind of country where ten kilometres can soak up an hour, and it seemed like an age before Chris slowed, consulted the GPS on the dash and pulled off the track. 'Probably better to walk in from here,' he said. 'No noise.'

'Yeah, good thinking.'

I waited outside while Chris unlocked a steel box behind the back seat and removed a pump action Remington Model 870 shotgun, charging it with half a dozen fat plastic twelve-gauge cartridges.

'If there's any shooting,' he said. 'This'll get us out of trouble.'

With the weapon slung over his shoulder, we set off for the river, following wallaby and livestock tracks through the scrub. The termite mounds were big in this area, some taller than me, made from the dull yellow sandy soil, still showing pock marks from the previous wet season's rains. The saddest thing, however, about the bush around here, was the demise of goannas since the arrival of the cane toad, years earlier.

Gould's water monitors, perentie lizards and a half dozen other species, some of which could grow to a good two metres, were all but gone, replaced by the fat hopping toads that we heard thudding off into the bush, ugly poisonous hides dull even under the sun. Introduced by the unthinking cane farmers of North Queensland, there were few things that made me angrier than the coming of the toads.

We heard the river before we saw it, the terrain becoming rocky with patches of marsh around each outcrop. Giant livistona – cabbage tree palms – grew in abundance here, giving the feel of an oasis.

The river appeared through gaps in the vegetation, the roar of running water growing louder as we approached. We had intersected the Roper not far above the third cascade.

'You managed that well,' I told Chris. 'It's just a few hundred metres upstream from here.'

'Not just a pretty face,' he grinned back, stopping to adjust the shotgun strap on his shoulder, before setting off again, following the river bank now. 'You get any barra in that pool?' he asked conversationally.

I stayed to one side and just behind. 'Lost one, first day I was here.'

'Good looking water, isn't it?'

'Yeah, that's what I thought.'

Before long I stopped to point out what must have been my own boot prints from when I had chased my boat down the riverbank. We looked together for tracks that might have been made by whoever had shot at me, seeing nothing obvious despite casting around for a bit. Chris waited patiently but then hurried me up. 'There's not much point in finding a few footprints, is there?'

'I guess not.'

'Show me what we came to see. That'll keep us busy enough.'

Reaching the place where I had first tied up the

Stessl and seen those smooth indentations in the mud, I bent over to show Chris. 'This is where they pump their water out of the river. I guess they wait until it's the last of the ebb tide when the water's fresh, then roll their hoses out and fire up the pump.' I jabbed out a finger. 'See the smooth patch there where the pipes were lying?'

'Yeah, I guess so.' He looked unconvinced.

I shrugged. 'It looked clearer before. Anyway, come and have a look, but keep that shotgun handy. We know they're armed, and that they're not afraid to shoot.'

Chris unslung the gun and held it in the crook of his arm. 'I'm ready. Lead on.'

The hollow paperbark was about thirty metres distant, closer than it had seemed that morning. This time, however, when I looked inside, it was empty. Not only that, but the ground had been swept smooth so that it looked untouched, even natural, leaves and bark strewn around inside as if they had blown there.

'Shit,' I said, 'there was a pump in here this morning, and a roll of lay-flat hose.'

'Yeah?'

'Of course, they've had plenty of time to move it.'

'So where's the crop?'

'Up ahead.'

Caution went out the window as I scurried ahead to show Chris what I had seen. There was, however, no sign of the wire fence that I had stepped over earlier. I turned to Chris, who had a worrying expression on his face, that *you are wasting my time* look.

When we should have been well into the plantation there was still nothing. Here and there I could see bare patches where something had been growing and removed, the space strewn with leaves and other detritus. 'This is fucking stupid,' I spat. 'They've taken everything. The plants, the fence. The whole bit.'

Chris shrugged, 'I'm glad we didn't get a team from Darwin down here. Might have been embarrassing.'

'It was here. I'm telling you, they were heavy with buds. All females. Bees everywhere. Whoever was growing them knew what they were doing.' Still I walked on, seeing hundreds of indentations where the plants had been only that morning. In the shade of a fair sized milkwood tree there was an area recognisable as a hearth. Someone had scattered the stones and tried to cover it over, but I could see where it had been. Nearby were scattered logs that looked like they might have once formed some kind of structure. A drying shed maybe.

Chris hoisted the gun back over his shoulder, holding it upside down by the butt. I wondered when he had last done a firearms safety course. 'Well, there's nothing now.'

'Let's split up and comb the area. They must have left something behind.'

'If you like.'

There was plenty in his tone that indicated that he considered this a waste of time, but he was a mate, and I could tell that he felt sorry for me. No one likes to look like a fool, and right then I had the dunce cap firmly around my ears.

We split up and crisscrossed the area, combing it over ten or more long minutes before I had to admit defeat. Chris had already given up, sitting on a fallen log smoking a crumpled cigarette.

'So what now?' I asked.

Chris smiled, the irony clear on his face, 'We walk back to the truck and get the fuck out of here. Maybe next time you're fishing you should stick to the water.'

'You don't believe me?'

'I never said that, but hell, Ben, I've got plenty of other things to do, and to me this looks like maybe a few wild pigs have been rooting around.'

I sighed, loudly. 'Let's go back. What's a few more kilos of dope on the street anyway?'

'Don't get the shits. What am I supposed to think? You turn up at Camp Leichhardt, word from town is that you've lost your head and needed a break, and then you bring me out here on a wild goose chase.'

'You called and checked up on me?'

'No, Ben. I talk to Katherine every second day. People gossip. They worry about you.' His voice softened. 'After what happened to you, who wouldn't go nuts? It's understandable.' He stopped, took the handheld GPS from his pocket and got a bearing. This done, we took off at a brisk walk. 'Hey, why don't you come over tomorrow night for tea? Susie will knock up something nice. I know you don't drink, but let's get together anyhow.'

I was staring at the back of his shirt, the sweat dampened fabric in the hollow between his shoulder blades. I envied him then. I don't know why, but I did.

'You think I'm crazy, don't you?' I breathed. 'That's what they said, wasn't it?'

'They said that you need to relax and enjoy your holiday.'

We walked in silence for a while, and finally the Hilux loomed ahead. Chris put the gun back in the strongbox and started the engine. 'I'm your mate,' he said softly, 'and don't forget that. I'll help you in any way I can.'

I smiled at him, and for some reason a tear came into my eye. Nothing he or anyone else did or said could make my life normal again. Nothing could. The Hilux eased into gear and rolled down the track.

We were halfway back to the main road when I saw

something fifty, maybe a hundred, metres off the track.

'Hey Chris, stop.'

'Yeah, what?' Even as he asked the question, however, he was already braking, not pulling over onto the verge, just stopping in the middle of the track in a billow of dust.

Opening my door, I stepped out, leaning on the door and scanning. The moving shape that first caught my attention had gone, but the scrub was patchy there. I looked back in at Chris. 'I saw something, I'll check it out and be back in a moment.'

Moving swiftly through the bush I saw a couple of droplets of blood, dark and heavy on the grass. Then I heard a noise – low, guttural, pained. I hurried in that direction, spear grass swiping my legs as I went, rounding the corner of a couple of stinkwood trees and seeing him again. Young. Male. Indigenous. No shirt, holding his face in two bloody hands.

I stepped forward, 'Are you alright?'

The hands left the face and for a moment I saw the extent of his injuries; both eyes puffed and swollen, nose bashed flat against his face. Red, slitted eyes focussed on me. His response was not of relief, but alarm. He turned to run.

'Hey,' I shouted. 'You need help.'

The would-be escapee managed only half a dozen paces before he tripped and fell, landing with a crash in the dry grass. I was beside him in a moment.

'Don't run,' I said, 'and don't be afraid. We have water in the Toyota. Come back with me.'

He made a half-hearted effort to fight me off, but then subsided. I realised that he was drunk. Very drunk. The stale beer smell on his breath strong. I was able to lead him back through the trees to where Chris stood at the side of the vehicle. 'What have we here?' he asked.

'Young bloke,' I said. 'Looks like he's copped a beating.'

'How unusual,' Chris commented. He walked to the back of the vehicle and produced a ten-litre jerry can of water. 'Sit him down, will you.'

The water must have stung, because when Chris poured it onto his face the man moaned and made as if to take flight again. He might have done if not for my hand on his shoulder. Half comforting, and half restraining. With much of the blood gone it was easier to see the injuries, the worst of which was an ugly cut below one eye and the badly broken nose.

'Do you know him?' I asked.

'Yeah, seen him around the community. Can't remember his name. I'll take him back to Gajiyuma, the nurse might want to stitch him up and set that nose. When he sobers up, I'll get a statement, but as you well know, Ben, assault is just a part of life around here.'

Together we helped him into the back of the Hilux, a can of coke from Chris's Engel in his hand, and a clean rag held against the injured eye. He watched me distrustfully as I lingered while Chris headed back for the driver's seat.

'Who did this to you?' I said softly.

The bloke said nothing, but turned and stared out through the cage.

Chris slammed his door and came back. 'Don't worry about it now, you won't get anything coherent out of him until he sobers up.'

'Don't you think it's a bit strange,' I said, 'that he turns up just near where I found that drug crop.'

Chris cut me off. 'For Christ's sake Ben, you're on holiday. From what I hear you needed it. Go back to the camp and go fishing, right?'

I sighed heavily, and looked at his face. There was no malice there. 'Right,' I said. 'I hear you.'

Chapter Eighteen

THAT EVENING I ran into the Yates boys at the ramp as I brought my boat around from its hiding place and loaded it onto the trailer. They were in high spirits, laughing and sniggering over nothing, drinking their beers and cracking jokes. Comments muttered under their breath were audible enough for me to get the idea that they were laughing at me.

At the top of the ramp I stopped to unscrew the bungs. The brothers were lounging around the cleaning table, watching a young bloke filleting an elbow slapper of a barra that must have only just edged over the legal size limit. He was making a hash of it too, hacking and sawing with a blunt knife, sweating and looking frightened that he was going to wreck his fish.

I knew that Terry and Wallaby Yates had spent the day removing that dope plantation. I wanted to kick their heads in. I wanted to arrest them and drag them to town in cuffs. I wanted to bring them down so bad it hurt.

Yet there was nothing I could do. I had no evidence. I ignored their smirks, climbed into the driver's seat and drove back to camp, hands and body shaking.

I cooked a fine dinner but it tasted like cardboard. I was worked up, full of anger and frustration and annoyance at myself and them. In the end I gave up being alone and walked down to see Konrad, past Maggie the biologist's van with its strange sounds and smells and the shadows of her doing something in there with her frogs and their foreplay.

I spent half an hour with Konrad. The poor old bloke was stitched up and sore, but one of the Nomads had brought dinner over for him. He was tucked up in bed with the light on. Not reading or anything, just staring up into space with that one good eye. The other was too swollen to see properly out of.

There wasn't much to say between us at first. Just small talk. Weather. Fishing. Some floods down south he had heard about on Radio National.

'I know about the dope,' I said finally. 'I know they're growing it. Maybe you can help me do something.'

'I am sorry, Ben, it is not my concern. I will say nothing about it.'

'I would have thought you might want to get back at them, for what Terry Yates did to you. What a bastard act, for God's sake, you're thirty years older than him.'

He did not deny it. 'All I will do is mind my own business.'

I leaned close to him, wanting him to understand. Like many cops I had no problem with people having a smoke now and then, or playing gardener with a few plants for their own use. When organised crime got involved, however, things got serious. Lives were ruined.

'Konrad, today I found a marijuana plantation. Those mongrels plan to make a lot of money here. Someone needs to stand up and stop them.'

He shook his head vehemently, his lips set in a tight, hard line. 'Please leave me alone now. I will mind my own business.'

I stood, looking down on him, still angry at what they had done. Konrad had come here to get away from laws and rules. There was only one problem with that. No rules meant lawlessness. Bastards like the Yates boys thrived.

On the way out I locked the door properly, and set off back to my lonely little camp.

Sometime in the small hours I opened my eyes. My fire had burned down to a smouldering ruin and had that dead hearth smell. There was no breeze, and stale smoke hung around in a pall. I coughed, unsure what had woken me up. Sometimes I had nightmares, visions of hell that I had learned to live with. Snippets of memory that were far worse than anything the subconscious could conjure.

Coming fully awake, I sat up, and then I heard it – the sound of feet across the grass – someone moving. I stared out into the darkness, using the old trick of looking out of the corner of my eye while moving my head.

It wasn't Terry or Wallaby Yates out there, but a slim figure, moving athletically. I came to my knees and waited. Even by starlight I recognised her – how could I not? She had a way of moving that was fluid and unique.

I staggered to my feet. 'Malea, what are you doing here?'

She came into my arms, as light as a breeze. My hand touched the sharp angle of a shoulder blade, then slid on to her shoulder.

She held the embrace for a couple of seconds then danced away and out of reach. 'You're okay?' she asked.

I felt shaky. My need for her was like an illness. 'Yeah, fine, what's up?'

'Don't worry,' she said. 'Ian is asleep. He was up drinking with the Yates boys until two o'clock. He was very drunk, and won't wake.'

Two or three in the morning is a strange time. A time when inhibitions can shift. More than once in my life I have shared a bed with a woman friend in all innocence, then woken at around this time to make love like animals. I felt it now, a sexual tension that would not have been possible during the day.

'Thanks,' I said huskily, 'for coming to check on me.' That was the only reason I could think of for her to come creeping through the night.

She grabbed my hand. 'Sit down. We are too visible, even in the dark, standing up like this.'

I obeyed, sitting on the swag, cross legged, almost but not quite touching her. 'So, what's happening?'

'I came to tell you something.'

'Yes?'

'Earlier tonight when Ian and the Yates boys were talking, I listened to every word. Normally I would not have bothered but they were talking about how they had made a fool of you. They laughed about you.'

I shrugged. 'That figures.' Keeping my voice low, I told her how Chris and I had found the plantation stripped, everything gone down to the last star picket. I wondered if she had crept out of bed just to tell me that I was a laughingstock with the local criminal element.

'Then they kept talking about tomorrow night. Something big is happening, and I don't know what, but they seemed very excited about it.'

'Where?'

'Downriver. That's all they said. They were whispering. Even when Ian is drunk he is secretive. I thought I'd better come and tell you.'

'Thank you. I appreciate it.'

Malea laid herself back, stretching out her near-perfect form on my swag, hands behind her head, staring up at the sky. 'This is beautiful, sleeping out here like this, stars overhead. Back there, in the Wildcat, it's like sleeping in a house. You are lucky to be so free.'

'I'm glad you think so. A lot of women would take the fancy caravan any day of the week.'

'Not me.' She sat up and made a choking sound in her throat. 'Damn you, Ben Mulligan. I'd found a small measure of happiness before you came along.'

'What do you mean?'

She sat up again and her face was close to mine. 'I mean that before I met you I had not found someone for whom I would risk everything.'

This piece of news was so unexpected that I didn't know what to say. In fact, I wanted to shout, scream, and beat my chest. This beautiful creature wanted me. It occurred to me that perhaps she would let me kiss her. Instead of making the attempt I said, lamely, 'You hardly know me.'

'No, I have not known you for long, but I feel inside that it has been years. Does that sound impossible to you?'

'No,' I croaked out.

'Lie down beside me,' she said. 'Look at me.'

I did as she asked. The swag was narrow, and my face so close to hers that I could feel her breath on my eyelids. I wondered what would happen. I did not have long to wait, for she reached out with her forefinger and did something strange. First she touched the tip of my nose, then followed it up to my forehead, explored my brows then down along the sides of my jaw to the chin.

It was as if she were blind, and had to touch each bit of me to feel what I was like. Maybe it was the darkness that made her want to do it. Maybe it was just some need to feel as well as see, as if there might be hidden hollows and places that eyes alone won't reveal. Fingertips brushed my ear lobes, then inside. My upper lip, lower lip. The slope of my neck, feeling her finger push lightly against the thick vein that runs there. I found the experience beyond anything I can describe. Finally, she stopped, hand moving to my shoulder where it gripped softly.

'When I was a little girl,' she said, 'I would dream of things – always escaping into a land of fairies and kings and queens. I had dolls and I would play games.

In my head I could be a princess. When I grew up, I found out that the world is not really like that.'

'No. It's not.' Hell no. I knew what she meant. Things are so simple when you are a kid, and maybe, for a certain kind of person they remain that way. For most of us, however, adulthood brings complications. Desire, jealousy, envy, and greed are still there, driving us. Things happen. Bad things happen.

'You make me feel like it is possible again,' she whispered. 'That there really is a fantasy land, somewhere.'

'A special place?'

'Something like that.' Her grip on my shoulder strengthened. 'The other day you asked me how I met Ian. Do you really want to know?'

I had a feeling that this information might affect the rest of my life. 'Yes, of course I do.'

I heard a pause; a sharp intake of breath. 'You're probably not going to believe this, but I was a fashion model, back in the Philippines. Even acted in some movies. Just as an extra at first – a shop assistant, a girlfriend, then supporting roles.' She stopped. 'You don't believe me, do you?'

Disbelieving her did not even cross my mind. If she had told me she was a goddess in human form, I would have swallowed every word. 'Of course I believe you.'

'You might think that the Filipino film industry is

very small, and of course it is compared to Hollywood, but over there I was well known.'

Malea would have made an exceptional actress, that much was plain to me. Not only was she beautiful, but more than that; there was something about her that made me want to be with her. There was sunlight in her. And I had known so much shade that this quality was irresistible.

'I grew up in a wealthy household. When I was a kid I was told that my father was a businessman, but I always wondered why some other girls were not allowed to play with me. I was nineteen, modelling for a Manila agency called Elan before I found out the truth – that my father's legitimate business front hid a web of illegal activities – drug trafficking, people smuggling, gun running. Anything at which he could make a profit.

'I confronted him about it and he admitted everything. Worse, he involved me. If I flew to Sydney, or Bangkok, strange men arrived at my hotel room with mysterious packages to place in my luggage. I was young. I hated it, but I would not say no to my father.

'Often, when my father would entertain overseas associates, he would ask me to play hostess, and to bring friends along from the modelling agency. One of the men who came consistently was an Australian, Ian Henderson. I knew early on that Ian was in love with me. He sent me gifts. Very expensive gifts. Of course, I was not interested. I had money of my own. Young, handsome men were constantly asking me out. I said no to him a hundred times and he kept coming back, trying to win me over.'

Using my elbows to prop my upper body so I could look at the darkened outline of her face, I didn't make a sound.

'Over the years, as I branched out into acting, I was able to lease a beautiful apartment in Alabang, the most exclusive suburb of Manila. My father, however, was in trouble. He fell out with some of his associates, and was betrayed by one of the high-ranking police officers he previously had on the pay roll. My father went to prison for six months and when he got out he was finished. My mother left him. His financial empire was in ruins.

'One night, Ian Henderson came to see me at my home. I offered him a glass of red wine in my best crystal glass. He told me that my father owed his syndicate five million dollars from their drug operations and that they intended to have him killed. Hit men were a dime a dozen in the Manila underworld. Such a thing was easy to arrange. I was doing okay but had no chance of raising even one quarter of that amount. Ian offered me an alternative. He would pay the money. In return?'

I grunted, fascinated. 'He wanted you?'

'Yes. Not just for a night. Forever. Marriage. To leave my friends, my job, my country.'

'And you did it?'

'What choice did I have? To save my father's life I became the five-million-dollar bride.' Her eyes shone with shame and sadness. 'Oh, Ben, in many ways I shouldn't complain. Ian has treated me well. Our honeymoon was floating around the Greek Islands in a luxury yacht. My marital home is a mansion in Toorak. I fly back to Manila every few months to see my family and friends. My father is free. Poor, but with his own place to live, and somewhat happy.'

There in the darkness I decided that I hated her father. What kind of man would let his daughter commit herself to a life with a man she did not like – a criminal, for Christ's sake? I hoped a fair chunk of suffering would come his way sometime soon. He deserved it. I said nothing of these private thoughts, instead saying, 'That's quite a story.'

'Yes.'

Before I knew what was happening her hands crept to either side of my face and she kissed me, gently and softly.

'I'm sorry Ben,' she said, 'but I hope you understand now that there is no way out for me. Ian would kill my father if I tried. Good night ... and be careful.'

I made a tortured sound in my throat. Already, however, she was standing. I followed her up, wrapping her tightly in my arms. She did not resist, returning my embrace with what seemed like real feeling.

'Good night,' she repeated, her voice unsteady. And then she was off through the night, leaving me bereft, broken, fat tears falling down my cheeks to the ground.

Chapter Nineteen

SETTING OFF EARLY, I told Chook that I was heading offshore to fish the islands. This was just a bullshit story in case someone asked. Instead I chucked lures up one of the creeks for most of the morning, a shallow, fast draining, mangrove-lined gutter that just about everyone avoided.

Two or three kilometres up, however, I found it quite fishable, particularly in and around another side creek, guarded by a big salty on a sandbar. Despite appearances I managed only one small mangrove jack, two fork tail catfish and an impressive surface strike that went no further than a nice visual experience.

By late morning I pulled up to the bank, and at a respectful distance from the water had a snooze in the shade, hat low over my face, mindful of the possibility of not getting much sleep in the coming night. By mid-afternoon I was back on the water, working my way, snag by snag, downstream towards the main river channel.

My luck changed. I caught and released three leaping, hyperactive barra in that session, all between sixty and seventy centimetres in length. My confidence returned. I felt relaxed and ready for whatever the night might bring.

As the sun set, I tethered the boat to an overhanging branch, with a clear view of the river.

Malea had not known exactly when and what to expect that evening, so I settled down to wait, nibbled a sandwich and drank flavourless long-life orange juice. The river, just before and after dusk, is never motionless. Things slithered around out in the mangroves, and predatory fish chopped at bait fish on the surface. Barra were easily identifiable by the boofing sound their big mouths make as they feed – like a bucket scooped through the surface of the water.

The insects kept up a constant cacophony, and somewhere, in the distance, I heard flying foxes on the move. Even at this distance I could smell them. An odour some people found unpleasant and others, like me, regarded as just part of the smell of the bush. The mozzies were bad here, and the only thing that kept them at bay was a thick layer of insect repellent.

As daylight disappeared the only sign that there were other members of my species on the planet was the moving pinprick light of a satellite high up in the sky, tracking through Orion's Belt. Otherwise, the world was its own, and nature ruled here.

Another hour passed before I heard anything out of the ordinary, the distant high note of an engine, coming from upstream. Few people were desperate enough to fish the river at night, so I had a fair idea that this must be them. Besides, I had heard the old Merc on three or four occasions now, and was familiar with the sound.

Starting the engine, I let her warm up, creeping along the hull to untie the line I had fastened to a branch. If I hadn't been watching so intently they might have gone past without me seeing them. The only light on the punt was a soft glow from the chartplotter screen, the men on board just barely illuminated.

I took no risks, letting them pass by the creek entrance before I twisted the throttle and pulled out from behind my curtain of vegetation. Gunning the motor, secure in the knowledge that they would never hear the Honda over their own screaming outboard, I waited at the entrance of the creek until they rounded the next bend. Then, driving out into the channel, I gave chase. Something told me that one way or another, tonight I would find the threads and connections that linked the players in this strange and complex situation.

Confident that my own electronics were screened from view by the console, I took it easy, using one of several previously established chartplotter routes to navigate the river safely. The tide was rising, the peak an hour away, so there was plenty of water over the sandbars and snags.

The boat I was following moved at a good clip, better than fifteen knots, about as fast as was advisable at night, particularly taking into account that I had five knots of tidal current against me. Tidal flow, however, is not evenly distributed across a riverbed, with back eddies, races and sluggish pools. Part of the trick is not to buck the fastest flow but to find the path of least resistance.

I'm not sure what warned me, maybe butterflies in my belly. The feeling that things had been just a tad too easy. Passing by a peninsula called Mutton Point I cut the motor, pulling in close to the bank, still moving along, but very slowly and almost inaudibly, scanning the long straight stretch ahead. Not only could I no longer see them, but I could not hear the screaming Merc, either.

I was beginning to think that they had simply passed on by, that I was wasting time, when I heard a soft voice out over the water. I turned, seeing the shape of the boat and men inside it, not fifty metres away. Even the dull glow of the plotter screen was gone and they had obviously shut it off in their efforts to check for anyone who might be following. Namely, me.

Minutes ticked down. Five, ten. They were being careful, but I can be patient when I need to be.

Eventually, as if they were satisfied, a match flared and someone lit a ciggie. What must have been a stubby bottle whistled out through the air, landing with a glassy splash and a white puddle of phosphorescence. Then the sound of the starter rope. Five, six times. A cough. A splutter. Finally the motor caught, revved madly before settling into a gurgling, erratic rhythm. A click of the gear engaging and away they went, straining until the hull planed, then roaring off down the river.

With a push on the gear lever and a twist of the throttle handle I was away after them.

I was not surprised when the other boat slowed and began to move into the channel that led to the secret lagoon I had fished with Malea. They had obviously charted the route well, for the vessel scarcely slowed as it tackled the shallows, surprising a massive school of mullet that erupted on the surface over perhaps half an acre of river surface, only to be disturbed again by me. One or two smacked into the aluminium bow, with a solid clunk that would have been audible on the other boat if not for the roar of their own donk.

The shadowy mangroves swallowed them up, to

the point where I no longer followed them visually, but relied on my own plotter to take me through. The chart did not actually show the lagoon, only a thin black line where I had gone before, over what appeared as dry land. Knowing, however, that there was no other entrance to the lagoon, I relaxed somewhat. I did my best to recall the geography of the place, even as I entered the narrow, mangrove-choked channel that would take me in there. The flying fox stink was strong here, and I could hear them squabbling nearby; their gremlin-like cries, shaking branches as they leapt from limb to limb.

The channel seemed much longer than it had when I was there with Malea, twisting tortuously. Once or twice I veered inadvertently into the trees, feeling mangrove leaves brush my shoulders, overcorrecting, relaxing once I was back on track.

Finally the waterway spread its arms into the lagoon, and out on the far bank I saw a fire burning: not just a cooking fire, but a good blaze that must have been designed to provide light over a wide area rather than keep people warm or cook food. I saw no point in continuing to follow the other boat, and instead made for the western bank, nudging the throttle up a little in an effort to be off the water pretty much as soon as they were.

The lagoon was a different place at night than it had been in the late morning and noon. Now it was eerie and strange, dark and mysterious. The main hazards were the trees that rose up through the ghostly water. Once or twice the hull nudged against submerged timbers, but an ounce of extra power was enough to free the hull again.

As the bank became visible, I pushed on into lilies and clumps of hydrilla. Keeping the throttle going I let the prop chew its way through, only cutting the motor a couple of metres from shore when they were too thick to continue. Mindful, as ever, of the danger from crocs, I spun the hull so she was beam-on to the shore and stepped into knee deep water, dragging the hull by the bow rope and making it fast to a spindly tree trunk. Taking only a torch with me, I crept along the spongy grass of the bank towards the fire.

Even at a distance the fire illuminated the riverbank so effectively that I saw the Yates's punt nudge against the jetty. What surprised me most were the numbers of faces out there in the night. Twenty, maybe thirty men around the fire and along the riverbank. Men of the Roper. A thousand generations old. Black faces and mostly shirtless chests shining in the firelight, streaked across with scars, bearded faces. Loud voices reflected across the water's surface.

Terry Yates dragged a tarpaulin off the load in the tinnie and, in concert with Hendo and his brother

Wallaby, began to unload, piling boxes onto the jetty timbers.

I quickened my pace, desperate to see what they were unloading. The boxes were the height and width of a concrete building block, and by the way they handled them, both heavy and delicate.

Men came from around the firelight to start moving the mysterious cargo up the riverbank and closer to the firelight, though at this stage I found myself having to skirt a side inlet, moving out of sight for two or three minutes before I reached the shallows where I was able to turn and continue my circumnavigation of the lagoon.

Soon I found myself close to the action, on the fringes of the last flicker of the firelight, and I had to move stealthily. At a distance of perhaps fifty metres I stopped behind a burned out tree trunk, crouched down and began to observe the scene.

The tinnie had been so heavily loaded that the stack of cargo was only halfway depleted. Closer now, I saw it for what it was, at once flabbergasted and surprised. I clutched at the tree for balance. Hendo and his bully boys were unloading, in the hundreds, the most potent toxin yet introduced to the north of Australia. Alcohol in the form of cask wine. Five litre casks of Coolabah Riesling. The cheapest form of oblivion available.

Casks of more than two litres in size were

banned in Katherine and Mataranka, with strict sales restrictions elsewhere, so the brothers must have travelled all the way to Darwin for this lot. Unless, of course, it came in via the yacht out in the Gulf.

My anger was such that if I had possessed a firearm at that moment, I am not sure that I wouldn't have sent a bullet through Ian Henderson's selfish, greedy head. Instead, I remained where I was, watching as eager hands on the bank opened casks, pulling the bladder out so they could be squeezed harder and fill tin mugs quicker.

One dark, bearded man held the cask high and sucked the tap into his mouth, squeezing the bag and drinking while the excess spilled out around his lips and over his bare chest.

For a quarter of an hour the unloading went on, the cargo changing to green cartons of beer, opened as quickly as they were stacked on the jetty. Then, finally, the punt empty, the three white men stepped out and onto the bank, beer stubbies in hand, joining in the circle around the firelight, laughing and watching the antics of the drinkers.

Those bastards were doing the unforgivable. Bringing alcohol into an area that was the only refuge for men, women and children who said no to the sickness and sought refuge in this so-called dry place.

Still, I could make no sense of what I had just seen. No money had changed hands. Why would they do it? What did it mean?

Even before the headlights appeared in the night, however, the pieces of the puzzle were already assembling in my mind. The vehicle came slowly, out of the wilderness, wheels stumbling on jagged rocks as it came down the ridge beyond the lagoon. It was a diesel, motor idling with a steady rattle. When it came into the firelight, I recognised it as an aged tray-back LandCruiser, maybe an FJ55, with the imprint of a hard life in the multi-coloured panels, scrapes and dings. The tray itself was piled high with sacks, and even as it came to a halt half-drunk men were swarming aboard.

The driver stepped out and greeted first Hendo and then the Yates boys. Leading them to the rear of the Toyota he opened one of the sacks, reached in and withdrew half a handful of something from inside.

I watched, scarcely breathing as Terry Yates produced a packet of papers and proceeded to roll a cigarette, using a generous pinch of dark green matter from inside the sack. He took two or three deep drags then passed it on to Wallaby, who did the same, coughed, then offered the remainder to Hendo, who refused.

The sweet smell of burning gunja drifted all the way to my hiding place. Hendo's plan was so simple. Come up here for six months of the year, set up half a dozen plantations in remote locations, show the locals how to tend the crops and dry out the plants, pay them in grog for their work. Boat the dried dope out to a waiting catamaran. When the boat was full, load up a huge caravan with another two or three million dollars' worth and drive back south. With only one cop in a four-hundred-kilometre radius it was relatively risk-free, and not hard work.

My only thought now was how to comprehensively and quickly stop them, how to smash the whole thing and get the grog back out of the community. Bringing these amounts of alcohol in was not just immoral. It was murder.

Half a dozen men helped carry the sacks towards the punt, where the Yates boys, giggling like children, were stacking the booty high. The work went quickly, and the sacks were relatively light. Even when they were finished, despite the bulk, the boat did not ride as low in the water as it had earlier.

Around the firelight, the drinkers gathered; shouting and dancing. To my tired mind they ceased to be men, but became lifeless automatons whose humanity had been taken away and made dependent on an insidious little chemical that has the power to take over a man, mind and body, until he is more slave than master, even over himself. A chemical that is destroying one new generation after another, leaving the next parentless and with few options than to tread the same path.

Images from my work in Katherine flooded into my mind. The unconscious bodies on the street. A town with a murder rate higher than Redfern or St Kilda. Bashings. Eye-gougings. Brother against brother. Husband against wife. Sick men and women in sick little circles. No one can stop a person who wants to drink above all things.

Now, here, the bush that had once been an escape was taking on a hell-like glow. The dance around that firelight was the dance of death. Already a fight had started in the shadows. Men shrieking, living in that moment, in that flush of inebriation where anything seems possible.

My eyes must have glazed over, for when I came fully to my senses Wallaby Yates was pulling the starter of the Merc over and over again, swearing loudly, the motor sputtering away for a few seconds before dying. Finally, revving the shit out of it so it rattled like a crazy thing, he jerked it into gear and they were away, leaving the scene of carnage that to me was more like Armageddon than the fringes of a pretty lagoon.

Chapter Twenty

THE POOR BASTARDS AROUND THE FIRE were making so much noise by that stage I was able to motor slowly across the lagoon, glancing back now and then to see them still writhing by the firelight, delirious with the false excitement that alcohol hides behind its aromas and textures and aftertaste.

I raised the outboard leg and motored through the shallows, deeply depressed, and beneath it all, damn it to hell, a desire not to run away, but to join them. To crawl, myself, under that blanket of forgetfulness and dullness. To drink until I could no longer think or feel.

Back out past the island I stopped the boat and attempted to get control of myself. This was serious, sickening shit. It could not be allowed to continue. Not for one day. Not even a minute. By the time the sun rose and set once more, I knew, people would have died for Ian Henderson's greed. You could not unleash such a torrent of free alcohol and expect nothing to happen.

When again I started the engine I had a plan. To get back to Camp Leichhardt and its mobile phone coverage. I needed to make a call. Get Chris out here and in a hurry. Not just him, but call Nev Hudson, the superintendent back in Katherine. That catamaran needed to be intercepted. Vans raided. Men arrested.

Back in the main channel I gunned the Honda. If they were waiting I didn't really care now. I could probably outrun them if I needed to. One thing drove my actions. The need to get back to camp and make the call. Besides, I was almost certain that they had turned downstream and would be making another run out to sea to meet the catamaran.

How dark that night seemed as I hammered the Stessl upstream! A light breeze puffed over the water, and the hull thumped a little as she hit the ruffles. My hands, however, shook on the tiller, and I found myself weeping into the night, as if only I and the dark slipstream cared for what was happening here in this country's heart of darkness where closed eyes have replaced paternalism.

The route logged on the sounder, the joined dots, allowed me to navigate safely at speed. My hands were tight on the tiller. I was angry enough to kill. How much money was at stake here? Millions, most definitely. For legal purposes a single dope plant has a calculated street value of one thousand dollars. How many plantations were in operation here? How many plants altogether? Many thousands. Perhaps tens of thousands. Incalculable sums of money.

Just upstream of the ramp I motored in, nudged the bank and tied off. I climbed the bank in darkness, again collecting a coat of mud on my boots, and walked downstream to where my Toyota sat in dark silhouette. I unlocked the door and pulled my mobile out of the glove box.

No service. I swore softly. The signal had, up to then, been reliable within five hundred metres or so of the camp. I climbed into the driver's seat and turned the key. Not even a click. I popped the bonnet, and with the aid of a flashlight from the glove box surveyed a mass of severed wires. Someone had been busy with a pair of side cutters.

Closing the bonnet with a metallic thud, I turned towards the camp, aware of that beginner chess player's feeling that the men I was up against were way ahead of me.

Mayor Davis's van was in darkness, but I knocked on the door regardless, hearing that hollow caravan rattle as I did so. The voice that came was tired and croaky, yet lacked the anger you might expect of a man being woken at midnight.

'Yairs?'

'It's Ben Mulligan. I want to have a word with you.'

'What about?'

'Something important.'

'At this time of night?'

'Right now.'

'Give us a minute.'

There were sounds of feet on the deck of the caravan but no pause for him to get dressed. Only a man expecting to get woken up sleeps with his clothes on.

He pushed the door open, clutched at the jamb for balance, then wobbled his way down the single step and onto the ground. 'Now, what seems to be the problem?'

I lifted my phone. 'No mobile coverage.'

'You dickhead.' Davis hissed the words. 'Who would wake a man just to tell him that?'

'This is important. What's happened to the signal?'

He made an exaggerated shrug with hands and shoulders. 'Who the fuck knows? Who cares? Go to bed, you dumb shit.'

Davis was an older man, but I was sure by then that he was as guilty as sin. I was angry, and tired, and in no mood to be condescended to by someone up to his neck in something as ugly as hell.

I grabbed him under the armpits, lifting him

clear off the ground. 'You've got about ten seconds to tell me what the hell is going on before I take your head off. Got it?'

Davis began spluttering. 'I dunno what you're on about.'

'Don't you? Start talking. Drugs, booze. What's your part in it? I've seen it happening. I know. You're gonna end up inside for five years unless you start helping me right now.'

'Fuck. Off.'

I squeezed him one last time for good measure before dropping him. He scrambled back into the van and locked the door behind him. I turned away into the night. I had no time to waste.

Malea must have been asleep, because she took a while to get to the door. Her voice was husky and warm like women's voices can be when they've just woken. I could even smell the sleepiness of her, and I wanted more than anything in the world to crawl into bed and hold her in the night and shut it all out.

Her eyes were dark as river pools. 'Ben, what happened, why are you here?'

'Can I come in?'

'Of course. You're white as a ghost, what's going on?' She poured me a glass of cold water and sat me down at a dinette the size of a pool table while I told her what I had seen.

She perched on the seat next to me. 'What are

you going to do?'

'I was going to call in the cavalry, but the mobile phone system just happens to be out.'

'That's okay. We've got a satellite phone. You can use that.'

There was something in her eyes that made me pause. 'I'm sorry. I know he's your husband and all, but he's doing something awful here. Really bad.'

Seeing her stricken expression, I put my arm around her, feeling the shivering tremor of her body. Her eyes were huge, vulnerable. 'What will happen to me if he is arrested?' she asked.

I felt a tenderness that was bigger than life or pain. This woman was now my responsibility. 'I'll look after you. You know that, don't you?'

'Yes. I know.'

We embraced, but she broke it off quickly, getting a black phone handset off a charging cradle and bringing it to me. I took it off her and got Chris's number from my mobile, knowing that I had to call him first, though I would have preferred to go straight to the top instead of dealing with his scepticism after the failed search for the crop. I did the right thing, however, and called, much as I hated waking a family man in the middle of the night. Surprisingly, it answered third ring.

'Chris?'

'Yes. It's Ben here.'

'You're up late.'

'You're not going to believe what those bastards are doing down here. I just saw the whole thing with my own eyes ...' The words tumbled out of me. When I was finished his voice went soft and, it seemed to me, resigned.

'It all adds up then.'

'It does?'

'Yeah. Things have been happening at this end too.'

'So you believe me about the dope crop now?'

'Course I do. Always did. It was just frustrating to go out there and find the place clean.'

'Let's do this properly,' I said, 'get the drug squad down here. Roll the whole thing up.'

'Absolutely right,' he said, 'and I'll call them now. But if you help me out, we can get some hard evidence tonight.'

'How?'

'There's another meeting, soon. That wasn't the only one. With you as backup we can wrap up a couple of the conspirators in possession of part of one of the crops. That would be worthwhile, wouldn't it?'

So one shipment was going out by road, I thought to myself, spreading the risk. 'It would certainly help if we could arrest them red-handed. Where do you want to meet?'

'Have you got a map?'

'Of course.'

'Just before Bullocky Creek Road there's a track that runs along a fence line down to the left. Three point five ks down, there's a cluster of boulders the blackfellers call the Turkey Eggs. Meet me there in half an hour.'

'Yeah, providing I can get hold of a vehicle.'

'Where's yours?'

'Every lead you can get at has been severed with side cutters.'

'Nice friends you've got down there.'

'See you soon.'

'Yeah, see you.'

When I put down the phone Malea looked at me with wary eyes, swollen and softened around the edges by tears. 'Don't go. I have our Jimni. Let's drive away from here. There is no need for you to do anything dangerous.' As if to illustrate her willingness to pursue the idea she opened a wardrobe and began pulling out clothes.

I couldn't think. I didn't know what to do. The idea was appealing. Before my amazed eyes she turned her back, unbuttoned her pyjama top, slipped it down through her arms, then clipped on a bra and white shirt. Then she did the same thing with her bottom half. Next a small suitcase appeared and she started throwing clothes inside.

'No Malea. I have to go with Chris,' I said finally.

'He's my colleague, my mate, and he needs me.'

'He needs you? No, he doesn't. But I do. You don't understand my husband. He kills men if they get in his way. He has done it before. You've already been shot at once.'

'I'm a cop. I have to see this through.'

'You're on holidays.'

I had to laugh then, just a chuckle. That line again.

'Come with me Ben. Right now, this minute.' Her body language combined with her eyes to plead with me – hands folded together below her chin. Head bowed. 'I'm falling in love with you, and I don't want to lose you.'

It is hard to describe how it felt to hear those words, and at first I struggled for a response. 'I feel the same way, but I can't go just yet.' I stopped, knowing how crass the next question was going to sound. 'Can I borrow your car?'

Malea stopped packing, walked to the kitchen bench and threw the keys at me, straight and hard. 'You stupid bastard. Just go and get yourself killed.'

If ever there was a moment when I might have changed my mind, that was it, and later, of course, I wished to God I had. Instead, a sense of duty – not to my job, but to natural justice – sent me out into the night and away.

Chapter Twenty-one

THE TACHO NEEDLE on the little Suzuki had probably never seen quite so much of the red line as it did that night. There was no traffic, just one road train careering down the middle of the road as if on rails, spotlights turning night into day and forcing me over into the verge. Poor bastards must hate all the driving, the endless roads, bringing a load of fats up from one of the Gulf stations.

So busy was my mind that I almost missed the turn. It was the fence line that did it for me, jogging my memory. The track was narrow and corrugated, with the occasional washout, deep and trench-like, that required slowing right down and full attention. I noticed tyre tracks where at least one vehicle had travelled along in the last few hours or so.

Finally, the headlights picked up the rounded rocks that must have been the Turkey Eggs. There was no one around. I killed the engine and wound down the window, listening to the slow ticking as the engine cooled and the night sounds out in the bush. While I waited, I thought about Malea. Of course I had wanted to go with her. I was captivated. I had never encountered her particular mix of femininity, physical competence and intelligence before. I wanted her badly – more than anything – but the demons in my mind were all bound up with the demons of this place. I had to lay them to rest first.

The sound of tyres on the track came before the engine noise. The headlights; yellow light – and LED spotties; blue light – lit the area like day, so bright I could not look into them. Barred shadows from tree trunks passed across the dusty windscreen. I stepped out of the car, blinded like a night animal confronted with dawn, still holding the door for balance.

The other vehicle stopped, engine running. The spotlights switched off. A door slammed.

First Hendo, then the Yates boys got out, one after the other, seemingly taller than I remembered. Wraith-like in silhouette.

My grip on the door tightened. 'Where's Chris?' I called.

'Oh, sorry,' said Hendo, 'he couldn't make it. What a shame, you poor fucker. You got me instead, and I have to warn you. I'm angry. You've turned into a pain in the arse.'

'If you've hurt Chris you are in a pile of shit.'

Hendo laughed, and I wondered why. 'I've been making enquiries about you,' he smirked. 'Thought you were such a holier than thou princess with your not drinking and all that shit. I found out why, and it's not that pretty, is it?'

I can take a punch as good as the next bloke, but this was a king hit that sent me reeling. How the hell did he find out? Who had he been talking to?

'Nice girl too,' he said, 'dead. Just nineteen, wasn't she? Tell us, Mulligan. Tell us why you don't drink.'

My mind fell into the abyss. The one I knew so well.

Oh Jesus. Is she alright? Tell me she's not hurt bad, please.

I remembered the paramedic's voice when I screamed it out to him, squinting out at the wreckage and flotsam of the crash strewn all over the road verge.

Voice deadpan. *Your girlfriend's dead, mate.*

Pissed? Yeah, been shotgunning cans in good old Territory style down near the river bank. Middle of the day drunk with a sun-lit world like streaks of liquid dye down the inside of my eyelids. Crying on the side of the road with blood running down my neck from a cut on my chin, flooding down my shirt. More cars stopping and people staring.

Then at the hospital, and there was a male nurse

wanting to stick a needle in my arm for the blood alcohol sample. I remembered then how the station sergeant, Grant Lewis, who had never seemed to like me anyway, rolled up his sleeve and said to the nurse, 'Here, son. Take the blood from here.'

The kid looked like he'd swallowed a lemon. 'I really can't ...'

'Just do it you little prick,' Lewis had said, and I'd watched the nurse take blood from his arm, and he stared at me like I was undergoing some baptism of fire.

His eyes said: Don't worry, we always look after our own around here.

Then, of course, the blood alcohol reading had come back under the limit. I was safe, and Sergeant Grant Lewis had draped an arm around my shoulders the next day like he was my brother, and I was off scot-free but a beautiful girl was lying dead in the morgue.

I had to face her family. Telling them I was sorry was woefully insufficient, yet what else could I give them? I had two weeks leave in Darwin wandering from the Vic Hotel to Lim's to the Casino, carousing with cops I'd known through training who had all heard what happened and didn't want to talk about it either.

'No wonder you don't drink,' Hendo said. 'You killed a girl. Drink driving. You fuckin' idiot. That's why you don't drink.'

I stared at him, wanting to explain. The accident didn't stop me drinking. It started it, really. Drinking to forget the thing that drinking made me do. That was when I really learned what grog can do to a man. How it deadens the heart and soul from pain, but, after a while, pleasure as well.

Wallaby Yates was getting something from the rear of the Nissan. I stared at the thing in his hands. The polished wood and blued steel of a hunting rifle. I was so dazed I didn't even connect the damn thing with my own safety. Just looked stupidly at the gun and wondered what the hell they were going to do with it.

I turned my face towards Hendo, and I saw something in his eyes. Something that meant death to me. He was going to kill me. The mongrel was going to kill me.

Death was not a strange concept. I'd stared that spectre down on more than one occasion. I'd considered all the options, all the ways and means and how it might feel; even stood in the shed near the rack of fishing rods with my hands on a coil of blue and yellow telecom rope and stared up at the timber beams and a chair and thought how easy it would be.

I'd held the Turkish walnut stock of a Brno Model 2 in my hands and touched the muzzle to my lips so I could taste the bitter salt of the gun oil. Listened to all the different corners of my heart state their case. Fear. Desire for escape. Knowing that somehow my punishment was not yet done.

The problem was that, sober, I couldn't escape the memories. The whiteness of the hospital and the crowds as the ambos brought us in. Doctors, nurses – and even then I didn't realise that they had given up trying to save her life.

Your girlfriend's dead, mate.

Oh, fuck, even now how those words scream through my soul and I see her the way I last saw her and I see the expressions on their faces. How I had taken her life in my hands, let her into my car when I should not have been in charge of a chair, let alone a motor vehicle.

Beneath it all, before and after, is the fog of alcohol. The thickness, the forgetting, the nights when I drank until I could not stop crying; mates sitting with me on the steps below the elevated upper floor of that house we shared while I let the grog take the twist-top off my grief, and the creamy evil smelling stuff inside drained out.

This wasn't the way it was supposed to be. This was supposed to be the beginning, not the end for us. This was not life, and most of the time I wished I was dead beside her on that road.

Six months passed in an alcoholic blur. Lying drunk in the darkness listening to music. Listening to the special songs over and over again, the ones that you think are going to explain it all. Only problem is that nothing can. Music goes closest, gets you leaning out close to touch it. When you're drunk you go closer still, close enough that your hands are out straight, quivering, and your fingertips brush against it.

In a blink, of course, it's gone, and you're left there, nothing more than a receptacle. No epiphany, just an awareness of your own mortality brought closer by the toxic soup in your blood. Confused synapses bringing on a pleasure and pain that leaves imprints on the soul.

I wished I had a god to turn to, but I just don't have religion in me. Haven't since, at the age of eleven, I spent a couple of months examining it from every angle. I decided that I could not believe in a maker, a designer, who sits plotting and planning, moving human hearts on a chessboard, sitting on a throne of gold. I could not believe in a heaven or hell. Only life and death.

Hendo pointed at me, 'Just shoot the bastard,' he said.

Wallaby Yates looked across at him. 'Are you sure? He's a cop. Dunno that I want a murder rap hanging over my head.'

'What else are we supposed to do with him?' Terry said. 'He's been sneaking around watching us for days. All we have to do is chuck his body in the boat and run him downstream from the ramp a few miles. Push him overboard and the crocs will chew him up. It'll look like an accident. No one will ever know.'

Wallaby Yates appeared to internalise this reasoning fairly rapidly. The gun came up and he walked towards me. I could hardly believe what was happening, and I remained there, dumbly, hanging onto the car door.

This halfwit was going to kill me. He really thought he would get away with it. I literally couldn't move a muscle, not one. Couldn't even blink as he drew back the bolt and I heard the cartridge slide into the chamber.

Chapter Twenty-two

'WAIT,' HENDO SNAPPED. 'Maybe it's best not to leave a bullet hole in the bastard's body. And we don't want blood in the Nissan for some forensics expert to match up one day.' He snapped his fingers. 'Grab him, put cable ties on his wrists and ankles then chuck him in the back. The crocs can have him fresh.'

Terry Yates said, 'But that means he'll see ...'

'Fuck it, he knows enough already. Besides, he'll be a corpse in a few hours. Get on with it.'

Wallaby covered me with the rifle while Terry ran in and grabbed me by the shirt, dragging me bodily out the door so I thumped face first into the ground. Dust filled my mouth, half choking me.

'Knock him out,' Hendo called.

I turned my head a few degrees, enough to see a rifle butt descend, driven by the flaccid but strong arms of Wallaby Yates. The butt plate struck me above the ear, with the impact of a kicking horse. The result was beyond pain. I felt weak with vertigo, and my ears rang. I wasn't unconscious but close enough. I made myself go limp. Someone peeled back my right eyelid. The voice came from a thousand miles away. 'He's out.'

They dragged my arms behind my back. I felt the cold plastic of an oversized cable tie, then heard the zipper sound as they tightened it. They did the same with my ankles. Two of them gripped the waist band of my shorts, then a handful of my shirt, and carried me to the rear of the Nissan; pushing and rolling me into the cargo space behind the back seats.

'What will we do with the Suzuki?' Terry asked.

'Leave it here, I'll take it home later. Then I'll deal with Malea, the treacherous fucking rag. I'll tell you one thing: that'll be the last time she does the dirty on me.'

They closed the tailgate, then I heard them get in. Three doors slammed. The engine cranked into life and we took off with a jolt, climbing through the gears with a strong whiff of diesel exhaust.

I'd expected them to do a U-turn, but whoever was driving hit fourth gear and stayed there most of the time, occasionally shifting down for curves or washouts. What the hell was down this way? Where were we going? From what I recall there was no vehicle access to the river, where they apparently planned to dump me.

There was, I remembered, a small waterhole

down here, some ancient Roper River ox-bow. It had an outstation on its banks, just a couple of local families doing their best to go back to the old ways. I'd visited once, and they'd been a healthy, cheerful bunch. Why would Hendo feel the need to go there?

For those first few kilometres I took stock of the situation, tried to relax my racing mind, and to see a way forward. The negatives were that my wrists and ankles were tightly restrained, I was in the back of a vehicle heading God knew where, and the three men on board had promised to kill me. On the positive side I was alive, and they thought I was unconscious but I wasn't.

My next thought was to investigate the cable ties. I tried my hands first, twisting and flexing to see if I could burst the plastic lock, but there was no give. Sliding one hand through didn't work, the lump of bone at the point of my wrist was impossible to get past.

Trying the same tricks on my feet proved futile, despite repeated attempts. I started to feel claustrophobic, close to panic, and my work at the cable ties was making me sweat. I rested for a minute or two while the vehicle veered through a series of bends, my body lolling as it went.

I raised my head, looking around the cargo space. My eyes fell on a battered steel tool box along one side. If I could somehow sit up, facing away from it, I wondered if maybe I could find a sharp edge.

My train of thought broke as the Nissan slowed down. Exterior lights spilled through the windows. I heard the deep hum of a big diesel generator. Voices.

The Nissan braked, and I lay on my side, as still as death. Faking unconsciousness.

'Check on him,' Hendo barked, and I felt the beam of a torch through my eyelids. Then a hand touched my neck, a sausage-like finger resting on my jugular.

'Thought he was fucking dead for a moment,' Terry Yates said. 'But his pulse is good.'

'Let's go then.'

The engine died, but I waited until the three doors slammed. Ten more seconds, counted slowly, passed. I lifted my head high enough so I could see through the side windows. This was most definitely the outstation I had once visited. But then I saw the shipping containers, at least three of them.

While I watched, a side door opened and a man stepped out from the nearest of these containers. A white man. He wore a gas mask, tearing it off as soon as he hit the air.

Hendo and the two Yates brothers walked over to talk to him. Wallaby had the rifle slung on his back. Of course, even he wasn't stupid enough to leave it in the vehicle with me.

They talked for a few moments, then the gas mask man turned and shouted back at the container.

A black man emerged, carrying a bag of white fragments. I knew instinctively what it was. Crystal meth. Ice. Shard. Terry Yates took a snort of the stuff up his nose, then handed the bag back to the man, who did the same. I heard them giggle insanely.

I should have been shocked, but I wasn't. My mind was numb. The scale of this operation defied belief. It galvanised me. Personal risk now seemed irrelevant.

I seized the opportunity, using my elbows to raise my body again. I turned my back to the tool box, and manipulated my hands so a section of cable tie touched angled sheet metal. Grimacing with pain at the awkwardness of the position, I did my best to rub the plastic through.

With my head half turned so I could look out the side window, my vision remained fixed on the five men over near the shipping container. It was impossible to tell if I was making any headway with sawing through the tie.

I kept working at it while the three men walked together across the ankle-high grass near the water hole. The man with the gas mask threw a blue tarp off something in the shadows, revealing a fully enclosed box trailer.

I must have been halfway through that cable tie when Terry Yates left the group and strode across towards the Nissan, heading for the driver's seat. I lay down fast, twisting my body and playing possum in as close to my original position as I could manage.

The front door opened, and the Patrol moved on its suspension as Terry sat on the driver's seat. The engine came to life, and the vehicle shot forward in first gear, stopped, then started reversing.

I guessed that Terry was backing up to the trailer, and this was confirmed when a new voice started directing him. 'Left a bit. Almost there.' A clunk as the tow bar must have hit the coupling. 'Whoa, that'll do.'

Wallaby left the engine running and the front door open while he went back to help hitch up the trailer. I knew that I had just seconds to act.

I lifted myself and backed up to the tool box again, desperate now. This time I must have found a sharper section of plate, for with all my force concentrated in my wrists and arms, the plastic tie parted after a few seconds. My hands were free.

I heard the squeaking of a jockey wheel handle as someone lowered the trailer onto the ball. The noise emboldened me. Speed was now my friend.

I pulled open the clasp and lifted the lid on the tool box, rummaging quickly. A pair of pliers came to hand, and I used them to cut the tie that held my ankles together.

I was free at last, just as I heard the clunk of the coupling settling onto the ball. I dived over both sets of seats, all the way into the front, twisting and turning.

I heard a roar of surprise and rage from outside.

Sitting down in the driver's seat I jabbed in the clutch, engaged second gear, and the Nissan shot forward. I heard the boom of a rifle shot and the rear window exploded in a shower of glass, fragments of which struck the back of my neck, stinging like needles.

Momentum closed the door, and I slammed the gear lever up into third. One of the side windows shattered. Something struck me low and on the side, like a sharpened poker driven through the skin of my abdomen. Sweat broke out on my forehead.

I'd been hit, I realised. Right through the fucking door.

More shots. I was only just past the camp, heading back on the track on which we came, when a tyre burst with the impact of a rifle bullet, and the steering wheel bucked like a horse. The Nissan slewed off the road and into a tree. My forehead slammed into the steering wheel. I opened the door, knowing I had to get out before they came up to me. I didn't know if I was dying: just spilling out onto the ground and falling.

I heard heavy footsteps and saw figures break the flooding glare of the outstation lights. With a supreme effort I found my feet and turned to run.

Twenty desperate paces on, the air exploded around me. A bullet swept past my head, leaving it numb, like someone had just stuck a garden hose in my ear and turned the water on full.

Still I ran, reaching some thicker vegetation, a pandanus frond cutting across my face. I ignored it, dropping one hand instead to feel the wound in my side, a slippery wet mess of blood. My breath sounded like the wheezing of a bicycle pump.

Another shot, and then the darkness swallowed me up. I blundered off, hand in front of my face to deflect branches. I heard voices behind me. My legs floundered. Hitting a tree trunk, I absorbed the impact on my elbow and chest, moving around and keeping on.

I saw headlights and turned so I was running directly away from them. It was some kind of survival mechanism. Deep inside I knew that I didn't have a snowflake's chance in hell.

Chapter Twenty-three

I ran as a disconnected series of parts rather than a single entity. Driving legs. Pumping arms. Heaving chest. Mind wandering, consciously forcing myself to concentrate on the now, keeping the past back where it belonged. As the memory of car headlights on my retina faded, my night vision improved, so that I could make out the shapes of tree trunks and branches in the darkness.

Ten or more minutes must have passed until I stopped, listening for sounds of pursuit. Nothing. Just darkness. I fell to my knees and turned my attention to my wound.

The bullet, it seemed, had entered on the right side of my abdomen. There was no exit wound. The blood still flowed, but thicker, clotted stuff. The whole area was painful, throbbing with each heartbeat.

Hell. I'd thought I was stuffed when I arrived at Camp Leichhardt. I giggled stupidly. Just look at me now.

After a while, I forced myself to my feet and started running ... well, shuffling really. My head swam with fatigue and shock. My life flashed before my eyes. A scroll of people and places. Mainly people. I saw them in my mind like a line at a bus stop. My girlfriend when I was fourteen. My brother. The old man. Mum. Friends. Enemies. As I watched them I wished that I'd hugged a few more people, and punched a few more too. There's no room for fence-sitting when it comes to emotions.

I saw a little boy doing up his football boots, taping the laces, and the old man pacing down the kitchen and telling me I'd be late if I didn't hurry up for Christ's sake. Loved his football, did the old man. Loved me, I guess. Mum hugging me and telling me to play hard and not get hurt. I missed them both.

I wondered why we have to have this hell of separation. People dying. People keeping on living. Why the hell couldn't we all be together for all time? Isn't that everything? Loving? Being together? Dying is a sick joke. Losing them is hell.

Nearing the end of my strength I fell heavily, breaking the fall with my elbows. I sat back against a tree, head lolling.

I remembered nights sleeping near the cascades at Galloping Jack's, with a young nurse warm in my arms and the river sweetness in my ears, hip settled into a hollow in the sand I had scraped with my hands. Fire smoking and rods leaning against a paperbark tree. Sand and stone, flying fox sweetness and itchy grubs in their silky strands under the freshwater mangroves.

Lazy breakfasts of bacon and eggs from the esky, and mid-morning have a few beers and sit on your swags and play guitars and sing, eating Smiths crisps from giant plastic packets while F18 jets from Tindal base thundered overhead. Mucking around in a mate's canoe, laughing, and trying to paddle, tipping it over and swimming shit-scared of crocs but the grog in your belly giving you courage and making it funny.

Swimming at night, lazing in the shallows letting the tiny fish tickle your skin, river sand soft beneath your buttocks. Neoprene stubby holder comforting in your hand and beer deadening the inside of your mouth and the whole of your mind.

Holding onto the roll bar of a tray-back ute, pig carcasses on the checker plate, just on dusk and the engine barely idling, eating up the ground with torque, and a mate beside you talking softly and drinking beer one handed and that's when you think that green cans are such a vital part of the experience.

I remembered my first attempts to stop drinking. Lasted forty-eight hours before I was back at Mac's Liquor down at Woolworths staring at the brand names, passing by the shining bottles on the shelves.

Jim Beam, Johnny Walker, Jack Daniels. I made my selection over five dry-mouthed minutes, wondering what particular recipe would best give me what I thought I needed.

I was drunk for a weekend and then I gave up again. Cleaned up the house, went fishing, came back and got drunk. Three months of oblivion.

Then finally, I stopped cold. Stopped crying. Stopped calling friends at three in the morning for sympathy. Began to put it together again. Worked my shifts without a quick trip home for a glass of vodka and a handful of XXXX mints.

I realised that if I didn't move soon I might die, either from loss of blood or from Hendo and the Yates boys finding me. I rolled onto my knees and as I lifted my head a wave of vertigo left me swooning, struggling to hold the weight of my head.

Where should I go? Which direction? East to the river then upstream would be the surest route back to the camp, or else west to the main road. Flag down a truck. How long until dawn? Four or five hours maybe. Was Malea going to be OK when Hendo got back? Would he take it out on her?

That last thought was the inspiration for me to use a termite mound to raise myself up, surface crumbling with the desperate strength of my hands. On my feet, finally. One step, then another.

There are no words in this mind dictionary of mine to conjure up what that night was like, running on through the darkness, following tiny erosion runnels downhill. Knowing that water would eventually show me the way to the river.

Mentally, I was like a dog with a selection of bones to worry and gnaw at – my own loss of blood and condition – Malea and what might happen to her, and finally Chris and what they might have done to him. How much was at stake here? A hell of a lot. Millions of dollars. My life. Malea. Chris. The lives of the people of the Roper descending into a hell of dependence and violence, fuelled on free grog and now, it seemed, methamphetamines.

At some point in that night I entered a forest, a place where trees grew tall and high, and the smells changed, becoming danker and darker until there was no grass underfoot, only sand and crackling leaves. I heard marsh gases bubbling out of still, stagnant pools, one of which I blundered knee deep into, almost falling face first into the putrid water.

The trees changed too, almost all paperbarks now: thick, gnarled old things that gave this place the feel of an enchanted forest. The bush is a different world at night – alone, with no light but a half moon – and in a place like this with trees that move and creak.

I slowed my pace, listening uneasily to the

silence. This was not just a place, but, it seemed to me, some deep recess in my soul – some ancient part of the subconscious, where layers of detritus build up and rot on the floor, becoming peat.

Ahead I saw the first of the glow bugs; fireflies, dancing in the air with their blinking white lights, coming together then seconds later drifting apart like sparks from a fire. As I staggered on deeper into this forest of knotted giants there must have been two or three dozen of them, one settling near my nose. I stopped, awestruck with the beauty of it. These insects are nondescript by day, no bigger than a flying ant, yet emitting pulses of powerful light so bright that they are dazzling in numbers.

It was strange that in such an extremity I should be touched by beauty, but as I walked on, I felt some new emotion that I could not put a name to. It was as if there was something sympathetic out there, something reaching out to me, and strangely, with the mingling of the loss of blood and the pain and fatigue, I found my cheeks wet with tears.

Still I stumbled on, and the glow bugs increased in number until there were a dozen near me at any given moment, hundreds more in the darkness ahead, lighting my way, showing me where tree branches twisted and intertwined; where fallen trunks lay, roots pointing barrage-like, uselessly in the air, arranged like the armaments of some long ago fortress, presiding over pools – water invading the crater left by the fallen tree. Life giving way for life.

Something ahead made me stop, holding my gut as I breathed, staring, bringing the hairs erect on my arms and the back of my neck. Through the trees, amongst the scattered brilliance of the glow bugs, was a greater light by far, shining a thousand times brighter, yet it too was dancing through the dark canvas of the night; constantly moving, erratic and lifelike.

The glow bugs and the swamp had been eerie enough, but natural, able to be explained. The sudden appearance of this light stopped me in my tracks. I had lived in outback Australia all my life, and heard the stories of Min Min lights – those supernatural, inexplicable beacons that appear spontaneously and indiscriminately. Even my own father had professed to have seen the phenomenon, in the thick Litchfield scrub, and told often of how his bowels had turned to jelly, at how the light held him in its thrall like a living thing. How it had loomed out of the night and seemed to fill all his senses simultaneously, creeping into his veins and chest as if infusing him with something beyond mere light.

This story came to mind as I remained rooted to the spot, and yet the apparition turned and appeared to move directly towards me, making an eerie, strange noise as it came – a soft crooning sound that chilled me to the spine. I would have turned and run but my legs would not move. Every muscle was frozen. Even my wound ceased to pain me.

I closed my eyes and waited for the light.

Chapter Twenty-four

THE LIGHT CAME CLOSER, brighter now, glaring into my eyes, blinding me temporarily. Soon, however, the whole scene began to unravel.

The light itself, I realised, was not natural, but was produced with a beam and a globe. This man-made device, in turn, was held by an arm, attached to a figure of medium height. One hand held a bucket and a net, the other a torch. The face was surrounded by hair, and the eyes huge, staring. The torch beam came to settle on me, illuminating my body and face.

Though half blinded by the strength of the beam I quickly realised who had half frightened me to death. Maggie, the biologist from CDU, out on one of her frog hunting expeditions. My surprise was so complete that I could not speak coherently, but reached my arms out for her, groaning with relief and surprise.

If I had stopped to think of my physical

appearance, of the blood that covered most of my shirt, and the grime on my face, I would not have grappled for her so suddenly. Instead of taking me under her wing and offering help, the woman in front of me let out a tremendous scream, dropped the bucket and net, and started to run.

Calling on all my reserves I sprinted after her, reaching her in a few strides, getting a grip on her arm and dragging her down to the sand, straddling her, feeling her buckle and fight. A contest of wills followed, that ended with her facing me, her breath coming loud and fast.

'It's me,' I croaked, 'Ben Mulligan. Please ... help me.'

She stopped fighting, 'Ben? Jesus Christ, you scared me. What the hell are you doing? You're covered in blood. Why are you wandering around here in the middle of nowhere?'

Talking was too much of an effort, but after shifting my weight off her, giving her space, I managed to blurt, 'Have you got any water?'

Seconds passed while she appeared to take control of herself. 'Yeah, my stuff is back this way a bit.'

Maggie led the way along the damp sand of an intermittent creek bed, laced with more stagnant, algae-filled pools, the remnants of the previous wet season. Finally, she stopped beside a grand old paperbark. Maggie's backpack hung from a low branch, presumably to keep the quolls out of it. From inside she produced a Franklins spring water bottle that looked battered enough to have been refilled many times. The cap was a different colour to the plastic ring that surrounded it. This she handed to me, and we both sat on a fallen tree, slick with moss, while I drank the first half, at which point I offered the bottle back to her.

'Finish it,' she said, 'I've got a thermos of coffee here if I get thirsty.'

I accepted the offer gratefully, draining the bottle before screwing the lid back on. Now at least I could speak. 'Thank you.'

'Would you mind telling me what the hell is going on?' she asked. I opened my mouth to answer, but before I could get a word out she cut me off. 'Actually, forget it. I don't want to get involved. I'll help you get back to camp though.'

I stared at her, starting to panic again. 'Can't go back to camp. They shot me – want to kill me. Have you got a car?'

She leapt to her feet, hands on her hips. 'They fucking what? You've been shot?'

I nodded. 'I think the car door must've slowed down the bullet or I'd be fucked by now.'

'Holy crap! Who shot you?' Then she sucked in

her upper lip reflectively. 'Those Yates brothers, wasn't it?'

'Yes.'

'They're bad people. Wallaby came over pissed one night and put the hard word on me. It was only when I went over the neighbour's van that he went away.'

My breath was coming in torrents, and I was fighting vertigo. I raised my voice, and I knew I sounded demanding, but I could not focus on anything else. 'Have you got a car, please?'

'No, you can't drive in here anyway, the bush is too thick. I walked, probably two hours to the camp from here. This is a dry creek bed that goes for miles. Sometimes I get carried away ...'

'I can't go back to camp. They'll kill me.'

'Kill you? Jesus. The main river's not too far down from here, but you need a hospital, if you've been shot ...'

I reached out and grabbed her arm. 'How far down?'

'I don't really know,' she admitted.

I held onto that arm like a starving kid onto a sandwich. 'Will you do something for me?'

A wary look came into her eyes. 'What?'

'Go back to camp. Tell Malea that I'll meet her on the river, tell her to bring her boat down. To meet me there, please.'

'Malea. You mean that rich bloke's wife? The young Filipina?'

I half breathed, half groaned, 'Yeah, yeah, that's her.'

'I suppose I can do that,' she said softly. Then, looking down at my side, 'Do you want me to have a look at that wound for you?'

'There's no time. It's stopped bleeding. Please, go get her. I'll wait for dawn then walk down to the river and meet her there. Please don't tell anyone apart from her that you saw me.'

I watched her pack up her things, and at the last minute she gave me her thermos and a trail mix of nuts and dried fruit. 'Try to keep the thermos for me,' she said, 'it's the only one I've got.'

Before she left I reached out for her hand and kissed it.

'Men!' she said. 'Bloody hell.'

For what must have been just a few hours I slept in fits and starts, devouring the coffee and fruit, but unable to stomach the nuts. When the sky lightened with the first gold dust of dawn, my side had cramped up. I literally couldn't move. The sun appeared, scything through the trees, bringing out the sweet and heady scents of what was revealed as a wide, dry creek bed, deeply cut from the landscape, clotted with stagnant pools and swampy ground.

Once, twice, I staggered to my feet with one hand against the wound to stem the pain, but was forced back to the earth, to lie on my back summoning my deepest reserves of energy and fortitude. The next time I got I up, I swore that I would not go down again.

Strangely, after a couple of hundred paces, pain, hunger, and fatigue segued into something resembling pleasure. The jarring of my knees and hips set up a springing sensation in my lower back, much like an underwater kick. The sun above, while it dried and cracked my lips, felt warm and benign. Now and then, I giggled.

Before long the creek bed widened, with more pools, surrounded by coarse sand and dry leaves. Clearer water in the pools now. I stopped to drink often. Up ahead a long-legged heron stumbled into flight at my approach, poor bastard thinking he had this hunting ground all to himself.

There is no way of knowing how long this period lasted, yet as the sun arced higher, the pain returned, and my breathing became ragged. No matter how hard I tried, how wide I opened my mouth, and how hard I inhaled, I could not supply enough air. My legs lost their elasticity. My knees became inflexible. I walked on rods of iron, with lungs of clay.

Not once but many times I sat down to rest. Could not prevent my eyes closing. Sleep crept up on me like a bandit. I forced myself up, talking loudly to spur myself on.

Finally I blundered onto the Roper itself, green-blue and beautiful, a sand spit extending from the creek mouth a stone's throw out into the main channel. The water was brackish here, so I could not drink, but I dug into the sand to make a small pool of water away from the edge; washing my face to try and stave off the dullness that threatened my mind.

The days of chucking lures into shady snags were just hazy memories as I struggled to climb the high bank.

My addled mind told me that I should move upstream as far as possible rather than just wait for Malea to come, and I struggled on, begging to hear the sound of her outboard, and to see the glossy white hull. That beautiful face.

Finally, however, I went down for the last time, and there I lay, too exhausted to move, think, or finally, to care.

Darkness came while I was sleeping. The sound of something slithering in the undergrowth brought me awake. My hackles rose, my skin becoming a mass of tiny pinpricks against my clothes, as if I were dressed in canvas. My eyes would not open. I could see nothing. Hearing, touch and smell were my only lines of defence against that frightening world.

Again something moved. An image swam into my head, something long, leathery hard and indescribable. Something ancient and uncompromising. I had seen many crocs in my life and my imagination was having a field day. I knew what the big ones looked like. Four, maybe five metres in length, wider across the shoulders than a stallion, skull so solid that a blow from a sledgehammer would scarcely cause a headache.

I knew the modus operandi, how they gripped a prey animal as best they could then slammed it up and down in an attempt to break the spine. I have seen a big bastard take a drinking buffalo by the snout and drag her every inch of the way back into the water until she drowned.

'No,' I screamed, my throat tearing like cardboard. The sound, the thing, retreated. But it was not gone. Oh no. Just waiting. Cautious.

I turned on my side, head resting on the muscle of my arm. Still I was unable to move. The place where my heart and soul now resided was warm and liquid, a flowing pool as seductive as hot springs.

I wanted to pray. But I have no god. So instead I prayed to the power in the sun, tides, moon and the earth itself, manifested in the flow of water and wind. I prayed to the endless force compared to which we are just moments in time. Pink, floating blossoms of memory.

The slithering giant thing moved closer, and I wondered if this monster was death itself. I could smell it, I fancied. The smell of carrion and rot. Maybe, I decided, this was my punishment, for what I had done. For what I am. Something on the dark side of cognition that waits to exact retribution.

Chapter Twenty-five

THAT INSIDIOUS CREATURE must have found the place where I washed my wound on the river bank, and followed the scent of my blood, drinking it from the grass and the air. That scent had excited the olfactory nerve deep inside its skull, transmitting an urgent signal to the tiny brain.

I knew the thing was coming for me. I smelled its breath again, and heard the drag of its heavy body on the sand. I could hear it breathe, and a hollow clicking sound deep in its throat. Fear and panic came in unstoppable waves, but still I could not move. My body was finished, drained of all energy. I had no weapon, no will and no hope.

Most crocodiles, out of the water at least, are wary by nature, and I was far enough up the bank to make it hesitate. Now, however, the smell of blood from the open wound in my side was enough to overcome all caution.

I braced myself for the attack, gathering enough will to drive my thumbs into its eyes, vowing that I would not go without a struggle.

Then, however, came another sound, so surreal that at first I thought I'd imagined it. Could it be a trick of the night? Another figment of my overactive mind. My name, over and over again in a high, female voice, echoing out over the water.

I gathered everything I had. 'Here,' I croaked, 'help me, please ...' I collapsed into sobs, wanting to believe that it was real, that I would be saved. I heard an answering call, followed by soft, light, running footsteps.

I called again, and saw stabs of light in the darkness.

This new commotion was enough to turn my enemy, I heard his feet scrabble on the loose earth, a rapid slide of rough hide on sand, and then a splash as he reached the water down below.

Branches parted nearby, and then a light. Finally a voice and a soft hand on my face. I sobbed gratefully. This was not death that had found me, but life.

Malea had beached the Haines a mile downstream and walked the banks all afternoon and evening, calling out and sweeping the riverside foliage with her Maglite. That wonderful, practical woman had worked her way upstream until she found me. Before long there was a fire to sit around, food in my belly, and fresh dressings on my wound. There was also a soft swag. Can you believe she walked back down to her boat to get it? I slept with this most beautiful of women in my arms, the fire warm and comforting nearby.

I woke in the dawn, clear headed. Remembering; taking stock. Cataloguing everything as either requiring immediate attention or shelved for later. My physical health was an immediate issue. The dull ache in my side. My cracked lips. Leg muscles that felt like someone had stretched me on a rack.

Malea woke also, kissing me gently on the cheek. 'I was sure I'd lost you,' she said. 'I almost went mad with the thought of it.'

'No such luck,' I grinned. 'Couldn't get rid of me that easily.'

'I'm serious.'

'I know, sorry. Thank you for finding me. I thought you were a croc.'

She pretended to slap my shoulder. 'I've never been compared to a croc before, but I guess it's one way of making sure of a welcome. Anything else would be an improvement.'

I focussed clearly for the first time, and I saw the puffy bruise under one of her eyes, and a raw lump on her lip. I tried to sit up. 'What happened?'

'Nothing, don't worry about me. Just lie down.'

'Was it Hendo?'

'Yes, Ian came back and turned the camp upside down. I told him you took the Suzuki keys by force. I had no choice. He punched me three or four times. I had to lie, if I'd told him that I let you take the car he would have taken me with him, or left someone to guard me. He is going to be very, very, angry when he sees that I am gone.'

I promised silently that Ian Henderson would pay for what he had done to her. 'Will he hurt your father?'

'Not yet. He'll try to find me first. But forget about him, he won't find us here. I've got something to show you?'

'Yeah, what?'

She picked something up and extended her hand. On a square of gauze sat a jagged, coloured, lump of metal. 'I found this in your side – not very deep – plus a few fragments of bullet.'

I studied it, amazed. 'It looks like a piece off the car door – shrapnel. Hell, I was lucky, wasn't I?'

We talked for a while, but she must have known how on edge I was. She took my hand and rubbed my knuckles with her thumb.

'Where's the satellite phone?' I asked.

'Ian took it.'

'Then all we can do is motor upstream to Gajiyuma. Find Chris and put a stop to all this.'

'Then can we get away from here?'

'Absolutely. Once it's in his hands I'm leaving.'

'And I,' she said, 'am coming with you.' Our eyes met, and held each other for a long time. Finally, she looked down and said, 'Are you well enough to walk to my boat?'

I spoke with more bravado than confidence. 'If it means you and I can go away together, I'll walk to Darwin.'

The Haines lay afloat on the tide, a little way up a side-creek. A school of popeye mullet were swimming in the muddy water nearby, heads half out of the water like beginner snorkelers, skittering away across the surface of the creek when we approached.

Both of us worked together to push the boat out, straining and slipping in the mud, then tumbling aboard, the motor starting on a shallow tilt and the prop churning salt water into froth with a helicopter rotor thwack on the surface of the water. Then, using wheel and throttle like an expert, Malea motored us out into the channel, settled down behind the console and smiled at me.

'You okay?'

'Yeah, sure. Thanks to you.'

Within a few minutes the river features became familiar, and I had a fair idea of where we were: roughly four river miles down from Camp Leichhardt.

I'd fished here what seemed like a lifetime ago, yet it was only a few days. The water was dirtier as the tides moved through the cycle from neap to spring, and there was more bait in evidence around the banks.

The flame of my fishing motivation, however, had died to embers and I paid little attention beyond that of habit. It was a relief to let Malea take control, to trust her enough to put my fate in her hands. She was good on the controls, cruising ergonomically, cutting the long bends, but never to the point of risking the shallows or snags.

Getting past Camp Leichhardt, when we reached it, was achieved with me ducking down out of sight and Malea cruising past at around fourteen knots. The Nomads were used to boats going past all day and it seemed the method least likely to arouse suspicion.

In the middle afternoon we reached the rapids where I had been shot at. Despite the higher tide, getting the heavy GRP hull through was tough on my wound, and for a while afterwards, motoring on up through the silent pool, site of the phantom marijuana crop, I found myself slipping in and out of consciousness.

In an attempt to keep me alert Malea stopped the boat and, using a neat little metho burner, made hot black tea in the shade of a grand old paperbark on the riverbank. There seemed little likelihood of anyone seeing us here, so we made no attempt to move away from the edge.

'Better take those bandages off and we'll have a look,' she said.

Kneeling while I stood, she unwrapped the bandages then gave me a few swipes with Betadine from a first aid kit. I winced.

'You big baby,' she chided me.

'Spoken like someone who has never been shot before.'

Watching her work, I enjoyed the gentle touch of her fingers against my skin. 'You were lucky it was just a fragment,' she said, and finished by planting a kiss on my side, above the wound.

'I'm lucky I found you,' I said. 'You missed your vocation. You would have made a great nurse.'

'Do you think so?'

'I think so a lot.'

Malea finished dressing my abdomen, let me drop my shirt, then got me to sit while she placed her palm on my forehead, obviously feeling my temperature. Finally she seemed to have finished with me, drinking her own tea now, sitting so close that our thighs just touched.

For a minute or two I stared up at her, watching the light through her hair, reaching out to touch it, fascinated. I had never seen hair like hers up close.

Black like those sticks of charcoal we used for sketching in high school art classes, yet so glossy it reflected light like a mirror. Rolling it between my fingers I wondered at its strength.

'What are you doing?' she asked, smiling.

I cleared my throat. I wanted to tell her something important. Something that I didn't think should wait. 'Malea. A couple of years ago I was in a car accident. I was driving and a girl was killed.'

'I know. Ian told me. He told me that you were drunk.'

I nodded slowly. 'I've gone over it a million times in my head. If I could change that day by giving up the rest of my life I would do it. But I can't.'

'No. There is no way of going back.' She took my hand off my knee and gripped it in hers. 'You need to find peace about what happened. There is anger in you, Ben, and it's all directed inwards. You have to stop hating yourself.'

'Thank you,' I said, and the mood seemed to lift. We talked for a while about what we wanted to do in the future. Listening to her, it occurred to me that forming a relationship is a process of fitting two separate jigsaw puzzles together. Sometimes the overall picture, or the colour, is just plain wrong. Sometimes the pieces are of different sizes, or the tabs formed of incompatible shapes. Just occasionally, however, everything seems to fit.

I got a tear in my eye at that thought, mixed with the stresses of the previous forty-eight hours. I wiped it on my forearm, trying to hide it, turning away until the need had passed. When I looked back at Malea she was smiling. Our thoughts collided. We both knew that we were going to be good together.

'Are you sure you're fit to keep going today?' she asked. 'We can camp here if you like.'

'Things can't wait that long,' I said. 'Free grog and methamphetamines, funnelled out into the communities around here. The results will be catastrophic.'

'How much further upriver do we need to go?'

I thought back to my earlier studies of the topo map. 'Eight or nine nautical miles. A few hours if there's not too much fast water that we have to get out and portage through.'

'Before nightfall?'

'I hope so.'

'Better get moving then.'

I must have been feeling a little better, because I remember savouring a glimpse of those beautiful brown legs as she stood up.

Chapter Twenty-six

ARRIVING AT THE RIVER near Gajiyuma after dark, we could smell the township long before we saw lights up on the ridge. Nothing unpleasant or strong, just a change in the air – cooking fire smoke, faint food smells, and a diesel generator humming away in the distance.

The first sign of life was a campfire on the bank with a drunken argument going on, a half-naked man standing, beer can in one hand, shouting abuse at a woman.

Malea moved to the far bank, idling past in the shadows, the Yamaha barely ticking over. We moved well past before finding a relatively clear landing place and then pulling up the boat, dragging it deep under overhanging branches so it would be difficult to see, in darkness at least.

There, beneath the living, interlocking trees we shared a brief embrace then walked away from the river. The moon was up, along with sprinkled stars and incandescent bulbs up on the ridge that gave us something to aim at.

Before long, I found myself struggling, and Malea took my arm. 'Not far now. There's a medical clinic here, isn't there?'

'Yes. There's a nurse.'

'There you are. She'll have a good look at you.'

All the way up we kept our distance from the houses with their outside fires and shrieking children, teenagers strumming guitars and the whole vibrant, confusing, chaotic crowd. Good people who need genuine friendship, and instead have been patronised, ignored, and drip fed with all the toxins of modern society without the evolutionary quirks to cope with them.

The station neared at last, comforting with that universal POLICE sign lit up at the front, though the neon sign was cracked where some vandal had pegged a rock at it. Chris's Hilux was parked out the front. I started to walk a little faster. He'd said he was onto something already, and I wondered if he had made some arrests.

The door was open. Solid, comforting Chris stood up from behind the counter. 'Hey Ben, where the hell have you been?'

I must have looked a sight, judging by the expression on his face. I staggered towards him, energy gone. Only Malea's shoulder kept me upright. I clutched at the counter for support, but then Hendo and Wallaby Yates came in through the interior door.

I didn't care. The sight of Chris freed me from an immobilising fear. To me, he was safety. Already I was blurting out what had happened, trying to open the little gate in the counter.

Just as it flipped over a big hand came out, connected with my chest and sent me flying across the room and into the wall. My body went as soft as that of a rag-doll. Malea shrieked. The room now had a sense of unreality about it. Everything happened at once. I tried to stand but a boot flew out and struck the side of my head. The three men came through and stood around me like a ring of schoolyard bullies.

Malea shouted out, 'Ben,' and tried to get to me, but Hendo leaned down and gripped her arm, twisting it behind her back, making her scream with pain.

'You little bitch,' he hissed into her ear, eyes narrowed, twisting harder so she moved her body in an effort to reduce the pressure.

Crawling like a beggar I tried to reach for her, muttering something incoherent in my throat. Again the boot flew out, thumping into my lower lip. I felt a tooth loosen in its socket and tasted blood, watched strings of it, mixed with saliva, drip to the sticky white lino tiles of the station floor.

I turned, staring at Chris, disbelieving.

His face had changed, twisted with anger. 'You had to come down here and stick your stupid nose in, didn't you? You couldn't just stay out of it. Now you're trying to fuck everything up.'

'You're part of this? I spat the words along with saliva and blood. 'You're going along with these criminals?'

Chris said nothing in reply, but his eyes said it all, holding my gaze, but widening, seeming darker.

'Why?' I asked. 'Why would you?'

The words came out in a rush, thick with self-justification and an attempt to smother the self-disgust he must surely have felt. 'Put yourself in my shoes. Try to raise a family in this shithole, with no end in sight. I want real money. I've got my eye on a nice little business over in Cairns. And you're doing your best to ruin everything.'

He looked away from me, then lifted that heavy chin and nodded to Wallaby Yates. I was still on my knees when that mongrel walked up with a billy club.

'I've been looking forward to this,' he said, and whacked me hard on the back of the head.

When I regained consciousness, my body felt as stiff as a four by two. The concrete floor was hard beneath my head and body. Sunlight shafted through the barred window. From outside I heard distant voices.

Kids playing. The world could be ending and children would still be chasing each other, playing silly-buggers, round and round, making each other dizzy. Laughing, teasing, falling over and running endlessly.

Seconds passed before I realised that someone was touching me. Their hands felt like snakes or spiders scuttling over my skin.

I did not understand where I was or what had happened to me. Fear and disorientation built into a convulsion that saw me half rising, choking out something incoherent at the same time.

Two people were in the cell with me. One was the nurse I had met a week or two ago down near the river when Big Billy was going off his head, the other was a young Indigenous bloke in a cop uniform. My eyes focussed on the badge with its twin kangaroos and the 'To Serve and Protect' logo. Two strong-looking brown hands reached out to restrain me. I let the man push me gently back to the ground.

He said, 'Hey, hey, settle down bruz. She's just dressing your wound, alright?'

'Where's Malea?' My voice sounded strange, muffled through a fat upper lip. It hurt when the damaged skin scraped across my teeth.

'Sorry. Don't know who you're talking about. Relax, we'll talk in a minute, I'm just as keen as you to find out what's going on.'

Lying as still as I could I let the nurse finish, then

sat up slowly. 'Thank you, that feels better.' I turned to the young bloke. 'You must be Eric, the trainee cop?'

'That's me. Who are you?'

'Ben Mulligan. Constable. Based in Katherine.'

'You're a cop?'

'Sure am.'

'Can you prove it?'

I reached down to my back pocket, surprised to find my wallet still there, but then, why would a criminal at Ian Henderson's level bother about nicking a few bucks? I opened it up to my ID card and held it up for Eric, who examined it, eyes narrowed.

'It's you, all right. What the hell are you doing in the lockup?'

I massaged the lump on the back of my head. 'Ask your boss. Where is he?'

'No fuckin' idea. I got home from court in Katherine at midnight. Found you in here bleeding on the cell floor. Chris was gone. Cleared out. Wife and kids too.'

'Shit,' I said. 'You want to hear something you don't want to hear?'

Eric wiped his eyes with the back of one brown forearm. 'Looks like you'd better tell me.'

Eric made coffee and we sat in the office. Kathy knocked up a couple of toasted sandwiches. I ate, drank and talked.

When it was over Eric looked at me warily. 'Earlier on you were calling for someone called Malea. Who's she?'

'The main man, Ian Henderson's wife.'

'You got something going with her?'

The tone made me bristle, but this man was on my side. There was no point riling him. 'I'm not sure, but it doesn't matter. She might be in danger.'

'You're the senior man here. What the hell are we going to do?'

'First thing we do is call in the cavalry, then grab the Hilux and find out where Chris and the others have gone.' My lips moved, but my mind was ninety per cent occupied with worrying about Malea. I felt a fear of loss that began deep in my bowels.

'The phones are out, I already tried,' Eric said. 'The Starlink modem smashed as well, and the mobile signal's out too.'

'The fuckers thought of everything.' I turned to Kathy. 'Have you got a landline over at the clinic?'

She crossed her arms over her chest. 'Yes, but you,' she said, 'are not going anywhere. Not for two or three days at least.'

I stood up so abruptly I almost fell, gripping the counter for balance. I felt a little sorry for her, thinking that maybe I had misjudged her. 'Sorry, but this isn't just about me.' With as much control as I could manage I made for the door, then turned back to Eric. 'Are you coming, or what?'

The clinic phone sounded static and distant, but I dialled through to Katherine and reached the duty sergeant, a recent Darwin transfer called Callum O'Hare. At first he thought I wanted to chat, but then caught the tone of my voice. He listened, dead silent.

'They fuckin' shot you?'

'Shrapnel from the car door and some bullet fragments went in my side. Nasty wound.'

'This is all dead set?'

'Absolutely.'

'Fuck. What do you want me to do?'

'I need men on the ground. As many as you can spare.'

'Hold on. I'll do what I can.'

With the wheels in motion Kathy stitched my wound tight and gave me a massive shot of antibiotics, then a strong local pain killer. Still protesting, she followed us out to the paddy wagon.

'You're mad,' she kept saying. 'We should call the Flying Doctor and get you to hospital.'

'No time for that.' I grimaced. There was no time for anything.

Last thing we did was go back to the cop station. Eric went in and returned with a pair of Remington 870 shotguns and a Smith and Wesson revolver. 'No point going in unarmed,' he said.

Chapter Twenty-seven

THE DRIVE ACROSS TO CAMP LEICHHARDT, with Eric at the wheel, gave me time to think. First I had to come to terms with the most disturbing twist of this whole series of events: the fact that Constable Chris Reilly was working with the enemy.

Why? For money, what else? Up until that point I'd met a few coppers who would pocket cash if it was pressed on them, or close their eyes occasionally to protect a comrade. Hadn't Sergeant Lewis covered for me by switching blood samples after my accident?

But up until that fateful night at the Gajiyuma Police Station I had never met a cop who had turned completely to the other side. Chris had seemed so straight. What flaw in his make-up had made him susceptible?

I have learned that some men hide their strongest character traits. A coward can be the most foolhardy in the face of danger, a brave man the most

252

prudent. A man with homosexual leanings can be the most homophobic. The greediest sometimes seems the least interested in the trappings of wealth. Was Chris Reilly's apparent nobility of purpose hiding a criminal bent?

I had to decide whether my feelings for Malea were real.

They were.

I had to be certain that Hendo and the Yates boys had really tried to kill me.

They had.

Where the hell were they now?

I didn't know yet, but thinking about the possibilities kept me busy all the way to Camp Leichhardt.

The track off the Roper Highway looked different to me than it had a week earlier. Back then it had been a refuge, a hole to crawl into. Now I expected only danger. The smells and signs of the approaching river no longer thrilled me, the pandanus and livistona palms taking on the role of harbingers, warnings.

One thing had not changed. Mayor Davis walked out from his dingy little van to warn us about the dust. Then, as he recognised the blue lights and police badge on the sides of the Hilux he narrowed his eyes, shifting from foot to foot and glancing behind him as if looking for somewhere to run for.

This, however, did not hold my attention.

Instead, my eyes roamed to the place where the big Wildcat had been. In its place I saw just dry grass and a huge rectangle of dust.

'Pull up for a second, will you?' I asked Eric.

'Whatever you like.'

I wound down the window as we came alongside. Davis glared at me as if he had just seen a ghost. 'You! What the hell are you doing back here?'

Davis looked like shit. Bags under his eyes like he hadn't slept for a week. My sudden reappearance had unsettled him, no doubt about that. 'Looking for some of your friends. Where's Hendo gone?'

'Wouldn't tell you if I knew.'

'What about Malea?'

'She's his fucking wife, isn't she? With him, I guess.'

'The Yates boys?'

Davis shrugged. 'They don't report to me, buddy. They do what they like.'

I took a deep breath. 'I am formally advising you that you are a person of interest in an investigation of criminal activities including the cultivation and manufacture of narcotics, conspiracy to murder and attempted murder. Please do not leave this area until you have been told you may do so.'

Davis blew air through his lips and gave me a look. Then, without a word, he sauntered off towards his van. There was no joy in his stride. My guess was that Hendo and his mates were about to double cross him, if they hadn't already. I wouldn't have minded betting that they'd promised him the world and delivered nothing. Even so, chances were that he would reactivate the mobile phone tower then get on the phone and tell them that I was on the move.

I turned to Eric. 'Keep driving. There's a bloke along here who'll know what's happened.'

Chook was out at the trailer, washing down the boat from a bucket of suds, husbanding the water carefully. He looked up warily as the Hilux came into view, but then, recognising me, put his rag in the bucket and hurried over.

'Ben! Shit. Good to see you!' He stopped when he saw my lip. 'Who belted you?'

I answered that one with another question. 'Do you know where Hendo and the Yates boys have gone?'

'Fuck knows. They all got back here late last night, started packing up. There were all kinds of things going on. They unloaded bales of stuff into the Wildcat, and plastic crates. They were gone before dawn.'

'Was Malea with Hendo?'

'Yes, but she stayed in the passenger seat of the F250 the whole time. The Yates boys went too, in the Nissan. They left their van here. Not worth hardly anything in any case. What the hell is going on?'

I looked at Eric for agreement that I should spill the beans. He nodded, and I went ahead. 'They were growing dope, and had a meth lab in a bunch of shipping containers.'

Chook slapped his leg hard. 'I knew that was it. The irrigation fitting and all that. Had to be.'

I looked up as Shirley came out of the van and gave us one of those looks women give what they regard as 'trouble'. Police almost always fall into that category. Now that I was in an official vehicle, I was no longer just a neighbour. I didn't blame her. Women usually smell a threat to stability and happiness long before their male partners.

I waved to her but continued to press him. 'You didn't hear Hendo say anything about where they were going?'

There are two ways south from Camp Leichhardt. One is back west past the Bar then all the way to Mataranka and the Stuart Highway. The other is to keep heading south down through the Limmen National Park towards Borroloola. This looks quicker on a map but is as rough as guts. Heaps of creek crossings, washouts, corrugations, bull dust; the lot. It would be hard going with a van the size of Hendo's.

Chook placed both big hands on the sill and leaned on it, forearms flexing. 'I saw them fill up some jerricans from the drums. Maybe they're gonna give the south road a try.'

I turned to Eric. 'Maybe they think they won't be followed that way.' It was lonely country, all the way to the Queensland border, at which point they could easily lose themselves in the tourist traffic around Lawn Hill and Burketown. The only constable anywhere near the route was stationed at Borroloola, and he would need to drive for a long way to have any hope of picking them up.

'How long ago do you reckon they left?' I asked.

'Three hours, maybe.'

I looked at Eric. 'You up for a trip?'

'Why not?'

I turned back to Chook. 'Have you seen my boat?'

'No, where is it?'

'Just up from the ramp a little way, tied to a tree on the bank. Would you do us a big favour and load it up for me? Just unhitch the trailer from the Toyota and park it here where you can keep an eye on it.' My vehicle could, I reasoned, sit there until I was ready, but the boat was a bit of a worry on the water, rising and falling twice daily, especially now that we were heading into the spring tides. There was, of course, Malea's boat to consider, but it was too far away to ask. I imagined that Hendo was technically the owner, not Malea, in which case I didn't care too much at all.

Chook nodded happily. 'Sure thing. The missus and I'll do it after dinner, be happy to.'

I smiled. Isn't it funny how you make friends of

some people and enemies of others in this strange old world? And that maybe if the good people are becoming your friends and the bad bastards your enemies then you must be doing something right.

We stopped off at my camp to pick up some tucker, a change of clothes and a few other bits and pieces. Our next stop was the official Camp Leichhardt fuel dump where we parked next to an upright forty-four-gallon drum, tilted so the dew ran off with a timber wedge under one side. A manual pump was screwed into the bigger of the two caps. With a deft cycle of the handle, the sweet smell of diesel in my nostrils, I proceeded to fill the Hilux.

Predictably, old Davis wandered over and started gesticulating. 'Hey, cop. You can't take fuel from there. It's stealing.'

'Shut your face, Davis. I am hereby requisitioning this diesel fuel for the Northern Territory Government. Send in a bill if you like.'

If looks were bullets I would have been shot ten times by the time Davis stalked back to his camp, but when the vehicle tank was full we topped up a couple of jerry cans that we found lying around. We had a long way to go, and didn't intend to travel at an economical pace, either.

By this time a crowd had gathered around. Chook and his wife, proudly telling everyone what was going on. People love to pass on news. The Trout turned up with his wife. Then Konrad, and a dozen others, milling around.

'When you get hold of the buggers, give 'em one for me,' said the Trout, 'dirty bastards. We come up here to get away from scum like that. Tell them never to come back.' Some of the others cheered.

'Go get 'em, son,' said Chook.

Even Maggie the biologist appeared from her van to see what was going on. I gave her a hug in the same way I might have hugged a sister.

'I lost your thermos,' I said, 'sorry.'

'Don't worry about it. Just sort those bastards out.'

Konrad cornered me also, gripping my shoulder hard like an old friend. 'I just wanted to tell you that I will make a statement for you, about what happened. You were right. Sometimes a man has to stand up and be counted.'

I looked at the old fellow with no little affection. His bruises had become angrier since I saw him last. I hoped to pin a hell of a lot more on the Yates boys than just a bashing, but it would all help, when the time came.

After another round of handshaking I jumped into the Hilux, considerably heartened.

When Eric let out the clutch and we took off in a cloud of bulldust, it was at a speed that I am very sure would have reddened Mayor Davis's face as he stewed away in his little caravan.

By smoko we were past the ruins of the old St Vidgeons Station homestead, chimney bases and flattened stone laying carelessly around the site as if it had been struck by lightning. Eric drove like a mad bastard, and I watched that speedo, knowing that even with a beast of a tow vehicle like the F250, Hendo was no way going to travel at half our speed. It was only a matter of time before we came up to them.

I love that country out there, down through the crossings. Rivers that I had fished, boated and walked. The Towns, the Cox, the Nathan; beautiful waterways, rocky in places and crystal clear upstream. Wild rivers that don't welcome strangers easily. Apart from a few private river camps, like Steve Barrett's place out on the Limmen, if you want to stay you have to find a spot for yourself. There are no shops; no fuel; no toilets; no nothing.

Just wild country with wild fish that fight for freedom just as hard as you hunt them. And that's the way of the world out there. Something's got to eat, and something's got to die.

Noon came and went, lost in my thoughts, but hungry now. I opened a couple of tins of baked beans, spoon feeding Eric as he drove so we didn't have to stop.

'Makes me feel like a big baby,' he said. 'For fuck's sake don't tell anyone.'

We laughed together and it felt good. Things were looking up, and the world did not seem so dark a place. When the tins were empty, I leaned back on the seat and tried not to ask myself the same questions over and over again. *Where was Malea? Was she alright? Had her feelings for me changed?*

Just after two, rounding a left hand bend I saw something that made my heart freeze. A woman, standing on the side of the road. For an instant I thought she was a hitchhiker, but then I got a glimpse of a man close beside her. Worse, I recognised the black hair and long-legged grace of her.

Chapter Twenty-eight

THE WOMAN ON the side of the road was Malea. Terry Yates stood behind her, holding a gun to the side of her neck. Parked just off the road was the big Wildcat van. I still couldn't see the carefully prepared trap I was walking into.

'Stop, for Christ's sake,' I shouted, reaching for the Smith and Wesson from the dash, checking that there was a round under the hammer. Eric hit the brakes and we pulled sideways into a skid, tyres crunching, sounding like they were going to blow out then and there. The cab rocked. Flinging the door open my boots hit the dirt, arm extended just like on a cop show. 'Put down the weapon,' I shouted.

Terry stared back. Showed me his teeth. 'Don't be an idiot.'

Whether I had not looked hard enough, or they had taken pains to hide, I did not see Hendo and Wallaby Yates until they stepped out from a patch of dense brush to one side. Both carried rifles.

Malea screamed out a warning, but it was too late. They had me covered. Terry's brawny, hairy arm tightened around her neck, and the gun jammed harder against her skin.

'Don't you hurt her,' I stuttered out. 'Don't you dare! Drop the guns.'

'You drop the fucking gun,' Hendo screamed back. 'You and your black mate.'

My eyes locked with Malea's. Her right eye was still swollen, with the promise of a real shiner on the way, but there were new bruises on her cheek and a fresh cut on her lip. They'd given her another touch up, the bastards. I felt an ache of tenderness almost at the same time as a cold burning hatred for the men who had hurt her. I wanted to start shooting, but knew that if I did, she would die.

The gun in my hand was now as useless as a lump of scrap metal. I lowered it slowly. I had no choice. I turned to Eric, who did the same.

'Good plan, you bastards,' I said. 'Add kidnapping and deprivation of liberty to the list of charges. You're really not very smart, are you?'

Hendo stepped forward, until he was close, covering my gut with the rifle. 'Oh, it's not hard to be smarter than you, Mulligan. As soon as Davis called and said you were on the way I had you figured. Knew you wouldn't be able to resist my slut of a wife.'

Wallaby Yates laughed, cut off when Hendo turned to scowl at him.

They sat us in the dappled shade of a salmon gum, uncomfortable on the crackling dry grass and dust. Terry lounged in a chair in the shade a few metres back from us, VB stubby in one hand, breathing fumes all over Eric and me, rifle across his lap. Looked like a Winchester, probably a .243, judging by the length of the chamber. It had a Leopold scope, 8 x 50 at least. Nice hunting weapon. Expensive too.

Malea was confined to the front seat of the F250, only once being escorted by Hendo up into the bush out of sight. A latrine stop, I realised, and on the way back I was able to catch her eye. Her lips moved and she mouthed something to me. It might have been I love you. I hoped it was. I mouthed it back. She turned away.

Time dragged on into the late afternoon. This was, to me, inexplicable. I saw no point to the wait. Why didn't they just do something with us and keep moving? They offered no food, no water, and I needed both. Wallaby Yates, however, brought Terry a sandwich, and he ate it noisily in front of us. When it was done, he amused himself with a tiny stick, impaling ants that swarmed to collect the crumbs from his lunch.

'You really are a prick, Terry,' I said.

He scowled. 'You should talk, dirty fucking copper.'

'At least I'm not exploiting the last people on earth that should be exploited.'

'Nah, just rootin' another man's wife. Trying to anyway.' He grinned at his own joke, exposing the gaps in his rotten teeth.

'It's not like that, Terry, but I wouldn't expect someone of your limited mental capacity to understand.'

He stopped torturing ants and swung the barrel of the Winchester to my belly. It is an ugly feeling to have a weapon like that pointed at you, the blue sheen of the scope lens, the black bore with just the suggestion of internal twist visible up close. I tried to remember what a .243 projectile was like from my hunting days. Probably eighty or ninety grains, the soft lead tip designed to fold over and break up on impact, forming a flattened mass that would drive through a man's guts like a twenty-cent coin moving at the speed of sound, churning and destroying as it went. I guessed that it was the same weapon that he had so nearly killed me with two days earlier.

'Careful,' I said, 'morons shouldn't play with guns.'

'Shut up, cop, or I'll spill your guts for you.'

Eric shot me a warning glance; why the hell are you stirring him up? To be honest, I had no idea, but it gave me something to do. Nothing much happened for a while, not until Wallaby Yates left the camp chairs and table they had set up beside the Wildcat, climbed into the cop Hilux and drove it off the road, parking it alongside us, getting out and opening the doors and back hatches.

Confused as I was, alarm bells rang in my head. That their plans were going to be detrimental to my own well-being was, in my mind, not in doubt. It was only a matter of how.

Wallaby walked back to the Wildcat, and after a short conversation with Hendo out the front, they went inside. A minute or two later they returned, carrying sacks of what must have been dope. These they stuffed into the rear of the Hilux. I'm so thick that I still couldn't work out what the hell they were doing.

'People died to grow that shit,' I called out to Hendo, 'people got bashed. Families were separated, blokes are in gaol. All so you could make more money.'

Hendo turned and gave me a sardonic grin, then returned for a couple of small bags of what must have been crystal meth, both of which went in the glove box. When it was done they came across, all three of them. Purposeful now. Terry stood up and covered me with the rifle while Hendo and Wallaby dragged Eric, kicking and screaming, across to a tree trunk and handcuffed his wrists over his head to a thick overhanging branch. It must have been hellishly uncomfortable.

'You dickheads are digging a deeper and deeper hole for yourselves,' I shouted. 'You'll pay, you know. You will have to pay.'

I still didn't understand that the hole they were digging was intended to bury me. That they had no intention of facing the music for what they had done. After all, they had worked for months, taken all the risks. Why would they let me take it all away from them now?

The Yates boys, one on each side, forced me down by the shoulders. When I kept struggling Terry gripped my hair and pushed down on my forehead towards the earth, so that the back of my head dug into stone and tussock painfully.

Hendo disappeared into the van and returned with two bottles of rum. I recognised the yellow labels. Bundaberg underproof. One of my old favourite poisons. A fighting man's drink. The cuddly, clever Bundy bear on the label. The smell of the cane fields of central Queensland. The reptile of addiction slithered and stirred in my chest. Even as I must have known what was going to happen, there was this thing inside me that welcomed it.

Wallaby used pincer-like fingers to force my lips apart. The lid came off the bottle with that sensual hiss of tin turning on glass. Then the bottle rim was in my mouth, and the liquid flooding between my lips, burning like fire. At first I tried not to swallow, but it was choking me and I was forced to do so in order to breathe.

How steaming hot the taste was on my lips, searing all the way down to my belly. They were canny enough not to pour so fast that I might vomit it up, but paused often. I kicked and struggled, but they held me fast, hands in my hair and on my ears, laughing like clowns but with sickly madness as I swallowed on and on.

I heard Eric's voice, strident and complaining, but there was nothing he could do. Nothing anyone could do. They had power over us, by weight of numbers and guns. There was no law out here. Not now.

Then came the bright dullness as the alcohol hit my brain, the first leaden pound of excited neurones telling me that I was under the power of this chemical. Even as the drug slugged me further and deeper into the forest of lost reasoning they kept feeding it to me. Kept pouring it down my throat until one bottle was empty and they started on another. It was sudden, and frightening, yet the more it went on, the more I wanted oblivion.

By then I was fighting for consciousness, and my vision distorted, my worldview altered. Voices became heavy and surreal. Hands no longer restrained me. I tried to stand. Fell. Demented laughter.

It became dark before I knew how and why. Time no longer passed in the normal way, but in a kaleidoscope of colour. Sunset, red and brilliant. A distant curlew. Wallaby footfalls, thump, thump, thump, out in the night.

I recall a campfire burning and a drunken, vacant laugh.

There was Eric, standing in front of a tree, and I laughed because I was wondering what they were doing to me – holding me up, supporting me on both sides and still my knees kept buckling and I wanted to fall. Gravity now had twice the strength. I was a mass of electrons, pulsing, lit up in the glow of a rising moon and in a world where all joy and hope had been stripped.

I felt the old Smith and Wesson police .38 they pressed into my hand, holding my right arm rigid with the barrel pointing at Eric. I heard the gunshot, and watched the red circle of blood appear on his chest, then another. I watched him sag down under the branch, only the handcuffs keeping him upright.

The blood is what I remember, in that crazed, drunken state. Jesus, so much blood. Then I was back on the ground, gravity claiming me, and they soaked my clothes with rum and forced still more down my throat

The last thing I recall was the sensation of gagging, and then headlights before unconsciousness took me into a blackout deeper than night and blacker than hell.

Chapter Twenty-nine

I REMEMBER ONLY FRAGMENTS of that night. Black holes and mountains. Places where self-awareness formed hollows in the depths of the mind. There were deserts. Islands. Clouds. Pinnacles. Lakes. Sunshine. Salt pans that drifted into the distance to merge in a shimmering mirage.

Sorry, I shouted, with all the force of my lungs. I didn't mean for her to die. One minute I was laughing with his girl. Then she was dead. I did not mean for it to happen.

Why has she gone, and where? Is there nothing that can bring her back? Can I ever stop the guilt that runs from my pores like blood and puddles and pools in the low places of my soul?

The constellations tracked their way across the night sky, and slowly my body began to metabolise the flood of alcohol in my system. Elements of my own self emerged. Sometime in that night my subconscious must have sensed a new, growing guilt among the well-trodden floorboards of the old.

Eric the trainee cop.

The muzzle flash in the night. The blood. Oh God, what have they done? What have I done?

Crawling through the night I searched on my hands and knees, bawling my drunken eyes out. I tried to call him but the words were a meaningless slur. No one answered, just the moon riding high over the ridges, and one of those strange night breezes. Still, on my hands and knees, I blundered into the remains of the fire so that the pain of the hot coals on my hands made me shriek. Finally, I touched Eric.

He was on the ground now, and whether he had fallen or they had released him from the cuffs I didn't know. I wondered why his skin was so cold and why he would not talk to me and why there was a dried crust all over his chest and body. And I could smell the blood-dead smell of him, yet even though I scarcely knew him I touched my lips to his as if trying to pass that indefinable thing called life from one man to another. Slumping to the earth and weeping, calling all the gods and angels of all the ages, all the figments of humankind's never-ending quest to explain itself down upon me.

I woke with the burning sun on my face and the sound of chopper rotors. When I opened my eyes I saw khaki. Cop uniforms, half a dozen or more. Voices. I tried to rise, but my hands were joined behind my back, steel cuffs biting deep into my skin.

Boots crunched on the earth. Something blocked out the sunlight. I felt myself seized, rolled over, and then my chin gripped between thumb and forefinger. I recognised the face that swam into view. A mate of just a few weeks ago. A man I had partnered with way back in what seemed like another life.

'You filthy murdering bastard,' he said. 'You're a disgrace to the fucking uniform.'

I tried to get to my knees, but I staggered, realising that I was still half drunk. My head hammered, and oh, shame, my first coherent thought was that I wanted a drink.

I tried to talk, tried to tell the man what had happened. Tried to tell him that I was thirsty. The only sound that issued from my lips was a series of moans.

'Lucky we don't put a bullet in your scone right now,' he said. 'I would if I was allowed to.'

I looked down and saw that my wound had opened. I was in pain. At least one of these blokes, it seemed, had got stuck into me with the boot. 'Haven't done anything,' I moaned, 'they did it. Took Malea ...'

'Save it for court, fuck ya. Save it for fucking posterity.'

I looked across and saw a black body bag.

Something was inside. A body, but the head still in view. It was Eric. He was dead. The dream-like events of the night were real. Behind him sat the Hilux, stuffed full of dope. The alcohol had me slow on the uptake, but now I saw it all. I understood.

They had set it up, then made a call on the sat phone, leaving me with a dead body, a pile of dope and a gun with my prints. Dirty coppers falling out. Oh Jesus they were way ahead of me. I had underestimated the bastards. Blokes like Ian Henderson didn't get rich and avoid gaol time by being stupid. With my past, who wouldn't believe it?

I was no chess player. Too much of a straight thinker. Twists and turns were beyond me, yet still, why hadn't I seen this coming?

The cops must have come in by chopper, and now they would be waiting for forensics, vehicles to arrive from Katherine. Then they would drive me back and I would be charged. Murder this time.

I heard them talking. Snatches of sentences. ... had a real problem with the bottle ... Chris suspected that something was going on for a while ... yeah, Eric was in on it too ... must have argued about the dope.

It was like a dream, some twisted vision that I was trying to interpret in the light of past events through the fog of that cursed poison in my blood. 'I didn't kill him,' I moaned. 'You bastards.' I strained against the bullbar my handcuffs were looped around

– the blood from my wrists was like slime, and crawled in ant trails down my arm. The cops stopped what they were doing and stared at me. I struggled to conjure sound from my dried out throat.

'It was Chris, the bastard,' I yelled. 'It was him, and Hendo, and the Yates brothers. They're getting away now.' I fell to my knees, my voice cracking and breaking into a series of sobs. 'You've got to believe me.'

They turned away almost to a man. My throat ached and my head throbbed. I wanted to die.

Somewhere in the wasteland of that morning, I must have slept, because I woke in the rear of a paddy wagon, my body rattling around and shaking from side to side. My head pounded and I had a thirst that would have made Burke and Wills seem hydrated. A sound system in the front belted out country and western music.

I sat up and looked ahead through into the cab. A cop was driving, the passenger seat empty apart from an iPhone and bottle of water. Through the front windscreen I saw the dirt road. The shadows told me that we were moving to the northwest. We were on our way back to Katherine. The dust we were driving into suggested that another cop car was a mile or two ahead of us.

They were taking me in. To the lock up. Or maybe

all the way to Berrimah Gaol.

Panic filled my head. In a matter of hours I would be charged with murder, along with possession of about ten kilos of dope and ice. I was a cop. The media would whip themselves into a frenzy. Trial by witch hunt. I had seen it happen before.

Then there was Malea. What would Hendo do to her, while I rotted away in Berrimah?

I couldn't let them get away with it. I laid my plans with care, waiting until the leading cop car was far ahead, yet still screened by a trail of dust that would leave them with no idea of what was happening. I wasn't cuffed – they had made a law about ankle and wrist restraints being used in the back of vehicles when someone had almost lost a hand from constricted circulation.

Looking around, I quickly worked out that this was not a standard paddy wagon, but a tray-back Ford Ranger with a cage only on the sides and back. I knew this one; had driven it myself. It did the rounds in Katherine as a utility vehicle, and must have been all they had available to drive down here today.

Taking off my belt and wrapping it around my hand, buckle foremost, I punched repeatedly into the back of the cab window. There were times in my life when I have been a violent man. I had thought myself past all that, but now it had reawakened in me. I was locked in battle with something far beyond a cartel prepared to do anything to hide their crimes. This was right against wrong. Good against evil. To do nothing was more criminal than to react with every fibre in my body.

The glass was the laminated, toughened variety, and it took twenty or more blows before it finally split. There was no way through, as there was a heavy grid of painted iron on the other side. Gripping a shard of glass between thumb and forefinger I cut my forearm, squeezed it, and spattered blood all over the window between cab and enclosure. It's amazing what the sight of blood can do. No cop wants to arrive at his destination with a dead man in the back.

A frightened face appeared in the rear vision mirror. I knew who he was. A young constable called Dale Cooke, recruited from Queensland. Mad fisherman like me. The vehicle braked and clattered over off the tarmac and onto the verge. Footsteps crunched on the road verge as he came around for a look. I lay on the deck, groaning and holding my arm, looking as inoffensive as I could.

I kept up the act until he opened the back door. Knowing that I would get only one chance at this, I went for him. He tried to move back but I grabbed his shirt to bring him closer, then got him in a headlock. Shifting my grip, I held the glass shard to his neck. I felt him shake with fear, hating the sensation but yet certain of what I had to do.

'I'm fucking innocent,' I hissed, 'and I'm going to prove it.'

I reached down and grabbed the Glock Model 22 from his holster, pulled back the slide then jammed the barrel into his back. He quivered, and I felt his knees almost give way. It was understandable. In my own mind I was a desperate man seeking justice. To him I must have seemed a crazed, murdering bastard, mad enough to slash my own arm, and almost certainly ready to kill again.

'As soon as I release you, walk away from the vehicle. Back down the road, got it?'

'Yes.'

'Go.' I gave him a shove in the back with my free hand and sent him stumbling off. He did not walk. He ran, making terrified noises in his throat as he went, seemingly certain that he was about to get a bullet in the back.

I did not waste time watching him, nor even closing the doors of the wagon. I ran around the side of the vehicle and into the open door. The engine was running so I got in and swung it into a U-turn, leaving my colleague still blundering down the side of the road and into the bush as if all the legions of hell were on his tail. The doors, of course, closed themselves.

Slowing down some distance down the track I bound the cut on my arm with a shirt from a sports bag on the passenger floor, switched the VHF radio off and let my breathing steady. Now I had time to think. There were two main barriers to my chances of catching up with the Wildcat that I could see. One was a police helicopter that was out there somewhere, probably back in Darwin by now. I tried to work out how much time I had before Dale Cooke was missed, found, and told the story of my escape. Then, how long it might take them to get a team into the chopper and back out here.

Four hours. Five if things went my way.

The second barrier was working out what the hell I was going to do when I caught up with Hendo and the Yates boys. This time it would be one against three, perhaps four, depending on where Chris was. I had the Glock, sure, and there was a shotgun lying across the back seat, but I couldn't shoot two firearms at once.

For the first time, on that desperate drive, I found time to grieve for Eric, a bloke who had cheerfully volunteered to help me, and had died in the course of duty. Out there somewhere was a mother, siblings, father, cousins, aunts, uncles, nephews, nieces – that seemingly inexhaustible extended family common to most Indigenous people. There was no solace I could give them except to nail the real perpetrators. From personal experience I knew that, in general, Aboriginal people grieve hard – take death hard – and when there is murder involved, they want payback. I was determined to give it to them.

Thank God there was water in that cab, a one litre bottle of spring water three quarters full. I didn't give a rat's arse about catching cold sores or chicken pox or whatever from the previous owner. I drank it down like it was honey, driving one handed while I did so, still keeping up speed, feeling the force of the Northern Territory Police bearing down on me from above and behind.

Careering around a corner at the summit of a ridge I almost collided head-on with a road train packed with multiple decks of cattle, the bovine stench thick even through the closed windows. Swinging the wheel violently back to the left I felt the Ranger go into a skid, missing the giant vehicle by inches, and finally coming to a stop on the verge, breathing like a mad bastard, wishing I could close my eyes and sleep, inhaling the last drops from the bottle of spring water and telling myself that I could not risk killing some poor soul driving the other way in the process of justice.

The water helped, dulling the ache in my head and smoothing the sandpaper texture of my lips and tongue. The better I felt, however, the more conscious I became of the death of Eric and the line I had crossed in hijacking the Ranger and setting one of my colleagues out onto the road at gunpoint. Even more now I felt the necessity to make up for what I had done.

To my pleasure and surprise, I caught up with the Wildcat just after noon, near the lost city rock formations on Nathan River Station. I topped a rise and saw the massive caravan ahead, trailing a shroud of bulldust that hung in the air for a kilometre.

As I pressed down on the accelerator and sped towards them, one determination guided me above all others, and that was to nail Ian Henderson and the Yates boys before they got away.

Chapter Thirty

CHRIS'S NT POLICE HILUX led the way. Then the Nissan Patrol belonging to the Yates brothers. The Wildcat brought up the rear. The whole cartel in one bloody line. Reality hit me like a pressure wave. This was going to be hard.

As I came down off the ridge and nudged up closer, the bulldust thickened until I was forced to flick the air conditioner onto recirculate and make sure the windows were closed up tight. The main benefit of the dust was that the occupants of the vehicles ahead would have no idea that I was behind them. I gripped the wheel two-handed, my mind racing, trying to come up with some kind of strategy that didn't involve a Rambo-style apocalypse.

The dust was not all to my advantage. It gave me no warning of looming terrain, drifting up on the windscreen so that I had to run the wipers to clear it. The tyres ploughed through puddles of the stuff, and plenty made it through into the vehicle, half-choking me.

I did my best to ignore it, speeding up until I caught a glimpse of the Wildcat's rear, swinging from side to side on the road, appearing out of the haze like the back wall of a house. Now was the moment of truth. Trying to follow under these conditions would wear away at me and the vehicle. I needed to act. Sweat dropped down into my eyes, stinging, mingling with dust and forming mud on my cheeks, while I continued to tighten my grip on the wheel.

Gritting my teeth, I swung out to the right. The difference, in terms of clarity, was dramatic, improving further as I reached the verge. Coming up behind the Wildcat, I switched on the blue lights and the siren.

The caravan and Ford F250 combination swayed dramatically. I had the advantage of surprise. They must have thought me safely on the way to the lock up, a thousand kilometres away in Katherine. Would they even know it was me – or think the police had finally seen through their plans? Ahead, looking past that convoy of vehicles, I saw a straight line of road for several kilometres, fringed to the east by rugged stone ridges sparsely adorned with trees.

The F250 careered wildly in my direction, the caravan following suit, forcing my driver's side wheels off the road and into the berm of road material left by the grader. I bounced viciously in my seat, my head hitting the cab roof with a thump. A twinge of pain from the unhealed wound in my side made me gasp.

The vehicle slowed and I had no choice but to let the Wildcat draw ahead. Again I settled back into the dust cloud – blind – fuming that I had given away the advantage of surprise for nothing.

Still driving with one hand I reached over the back and grabbed the shotgun stock, dragging it through the gap between the seats, then the box of cartridges. Flicking my eyes between the road and the task at hand I slid six heavy plastic and brass cylinders into the tube magazine with one hand. Twelve-gauge buckshot. Designed to rip through tissue and penetrate deep. Police standard procedure has always been to kill, not maim, working on the assumption that if things are serious enough to require shooting, you better put the bastards out of action, not just wing them.

I worked the pump, and laid the gun across my lap while I concentrated on the wheel and accelerator, edging up again. This time, almost the moment I pulled out, I saw a white Britz Troopie speeding towards me from the south, forcing me to swing back in violently. I had a view of two frightened Scandinavian faces and then I was clear.

I veered back out, taking advantage of the space

created by the passing car. Again I swung off the road, out of the dust and away from the pendulum swings of the van. The verge was clear of trees here, just low grasses and some rocks.

Winding down the passenger window, I rested the shotgun forestock on the sill. It was an awkward angle but I manoeuvred the weapon as best I could so it pointed at the rear offside tyre of the Wildcat. The butt thumped painfully against the crook of my bicep and a pattern of shot appeared on the rear panel of the van. I racked the gun and tried again. This time I was on the money. The tyre deflated and shredded. The van careened wildly then steadied, creeping over the verge as far as possible in an attempt to force me to back off. Ahead the road curved to the right, trees growing on the verge.

Changing my aim, I went for the front tyre. I got it on the first shot and that was it. The Wildcat rocked, and slid along on the rims, lurching like a down-and-out bastard, raising an even thicker pall of dust that settled out behind us.

Then, in sickening, slow motion, the whole combination began to roll. The van first, then the F250. Once it had begun it happened quickly. The Wildcat went onto its side and the aluminium panels began to disintegrate. I felt it inside as if it were happening to me.

My cold heart was already telling me that I had

just killed the woman I loved. That if Malea was in the van she would be dead by the time that giant sliding contraption came to a standstill. Aloneness, the absence of her, was the worst fate I could conceive of at that moment. Fear took my breath away as I waited for the Wildcat to stop sliding.

Eight or nine tonnes, however, of gross weight takes a long time to stop, even with the drag of the road surface. I opened my mouth and screamed, feeling inside me that barrel roll terror, and the hell of impending death, knowing that life and death can be the difference of inches, the result of an instant of carelessness.

The Wildcat slid to a halt half resting against a tree, the F250 on its roof, looking like a dog shot dead with windows cracked and starred and one shredded tyre still spinning, the underside a mass of dust-stained iron. Hell could not have looked so final to me, so frightening.

The expression 'heart in my mouth' applied to everything: heart, lungs, stomach, intestine all rising through my throat, and into the dry cave of my mouth. The cop Hilux had stopped now too, but I did not move a muscle. I knew that Malea was inside the wrecked Wildcat. I remembered what it was like to weep over a body.

I gripped the door handle and triggered the lock, staggering out onto the road, regaining my balance, hardly taking the first step when the air split with the concussion of a passing gun shot, and I had no choice but to dive behind the protective body of the Ranger.

My heart beat like a metronome. I imagined Malea bleeding to death while I was pinned down by the shooter.

Raising my head over the bonnet to look, the dust cleared sufficiently that I saw Wallaby Yates with his rifle resting on the door of the Nissan, thirty or forty yards up the road. He fired again and the bullet struck the front screen, punching a hole through it and taking a bigger chunk out of the rear passenger window just behind me.

I opened the nearest door and slid the shotgun out, holding it steady, watching the F250, from which there seemed to be no movement at all.

'They need help,' I screamed. 'Let me go to them.'

'Get in the fuckin' car and drive off,' Yates yelled back.

Before I could answer I heard the sound of an engine accelerating and I watched the lead vehicle, Chris Reilly's police twin cab, swing out onto the road and race away towards Borroloola and the Queensland border. The coward. Bailing out on them, and me. This event seemed to shock Wallaby Yates into silence.

'That's your brother in there,' I yelled. 'He might be bleeding to death.'

Wallaby Yates's voice cracked. 'You did it, you fucker, you made them crash.' This outburst was followed by a fusillade of shots, one after the other, thumping into the body work of the car. I kept low, relying on the engine block to protect me, knowing that I was safe there, but also that every second might be precious.

Still there was no sound from the Wildcat. Not a whisper; no crying, no sobbing. Images flashed into my mind. Where was the police chopper? Surely they would have been able to refuel and get back from Darwin by now. They should be here.

I tried to take control of myself. There was no one else, only me, and Malea was either dead or dying in that smashed-up vehicle a stone's throw from where I crouched. Only Wallaby Yates stood between me and helping her.

I risked a look at the Nissan, studying his position carefully. He too was crouching, using the open door as cover, the rifle now resting on the window sill. The door would stop shotgun pellets, sure, but down below I could see the folded knee and legs. I pulled my head in just as he fired again, hearing the crack of the passing bullet.

The range was long for a shotgun, so, safely back under cover I pushed the butt of the gun away from me and examined the muzzle. The Remington Model 870 has a choke at the end of the barrel, which works like the nozzle on a hose to control the pattern and spread of shot. I began to twist and manipulate the mechanism. For close work a wide 'spray' pattern is best, but now, for long range punch I wanted the shot to travel in a concentrated group, moving together so that as many pellets as possible struck the target.

Ready now, I leaned against the side of the vehicle body as if waiting for some invisible signal. I counted to five, I don't know why, maybe just in an effort to steel myself.

1,2,3,4 ...

I whipped my body upwards, threw the barrel across the bonnet as a rest, and lined the foresight up on Wallaby Yates's legs. I fired, the gun booming and the butt thumping hard against my shoulder.

I heard a scream of pain, and then I was running, the gun held at my hip, ready to fire again if he came up shooting. He didn't, and I found him behind the vehicle door, writhing and shrieking on the ground, trying to hold a dozen places in his legs that now leaked blood. Bone chips were visible on the surface of one of the wounds. I was tempted to shoot again, to finish him, but he was disabled, there was no need to do it.

I picked the rifle up from where he had dropped it, lifting it by the stock and smashing it down against the body of the Nissan until the soft carbon steel of the barrel was bent and useless.

Then, stepping over the wounded man I ran for the upside-down F250. The far door was already open and I ran to that side, noticing a wide blood stain on the dust near the door. Heedless of broken glass I started to crawl inside, half expecting to see bodies hanging from their seat belts like carcasses at a slaughterhouse.

Instead, there was only blood on the driver's seat and the dash. No bodies. Nothing. Malea, I suspected, might have been riding in the van itself. I crawled back out the way I came and then walked around the front of the van trying to work out how to access the interior.

I stopped short at a crazed laugh from Wallaby Yates, who was dragging himself towards me, leaving a snail trail of blood on the road surface.

'They've gone,' he cackled. 'That's why ... I stayed... to give them time to get away. Thought it was a whole bunch of cops ... was only you.'

'Where have they gone?'

Wallaby Yates pointed to the eastern horizon, a wasteland of tall sandstone pillars, eroded into weird and otherworldly shapes by millions of years of wind and water. 'Out there,' he laughed. 'Where you'll never find them.'

Chapter Thirty-one

WALLABY YATES FOUGHT ME every inch of the way as I bound his wrists, then his bloody ankles, with XOS cable ties I'd found in the glove box of the Ranger. Someone would be along soon, and already the flow of blood had reduced to a trickle. He was in no danger of bleeding to death.

He sat in the dust, half on his side, cursing me to high heaven while I went back to the Wildcat, where the water tank was dripping away. I filled my water bottle, drinking the lot in four or five mouthfuls. From the Ranger I slipped four twelve-gauge cartridges into each pocket. Then, around the door I found first one footprint, then another, heading off to the east.

To the sound of Wallaby Yates's mad ravings I set off into the bush.

Tracking is an art form, and the world's best are the Indigenous people of Australia. When I was eight my father had employed two tall, strong, but bean-thin Larrakeyah men to help carry his surveying equipment: the old theodolite in its heavy leather case, the tripod, and cameras.

Sometimes his job would take him into the bush for weeks at a time, surveying hundreds of miles of station boundaries, or new rural subdivisions. In the school holidays I would go bush with the team, riding up front in the old Land Rover. Camped along some water hole or other, Joe and Harry would fill the empty hours teaching me how to hunt, how to fish, but most importantly, how to track.

They showed me how a man leaves a record of his passing not just on soft earth where any fool – even, they laughed, a clumsy white man – could find it, but with bent over grass stalks, scuffed leaves, soft powder on stone. They taught me that a heavily laden man walks on his heels, and a quick man on his toes. A hungry man walks slowly, looking for food as he goes. A hunted man hurries, and hurrying men make mistakes.

I knew within a few yards that I was following three people. One small and athletic, wearing running shoes around size seven – Malea. Another not much heavier but with longer feet – Hendo. The third was bigger – surely Terry Yates. None walked with any obvious weight shift – to favour one side or other is a common sign of injury, yet one of them was bleeding.

Two or three hundred paces into the bush I found a heavy blood drop.

The sign remained sure and clear until I reached the first of many sandstone pillars that rose like sculptures from the tussocks and orange dust. Some reared twenty, fifty metres, higher than the eucalypt trees, with shaped tops that looked like old men's faces, bottles, or even women's bodies. The lost city of Nathan River.

The stone surface was not uniform in colour, but mottled with oxides, moulds and lichens, giving definition to the shapes. The shadow of an eye socket, the flush of a cheek. Dawn. An angel's wings. Breasts. Demonic, glaring eyes. Death.

Sometimes the pillars were widely spaced, others so close that I had to clamber up and over shelves of sandstone to get through. Here and there I found the marks I needed to keep me on the trail, grass smeared against rock, or more blood. I tried to guess the intent behind their direction, which seemed haphazard.

I was tired, and my head pounded. The aimless pursuit seemed to go ever deeper into the lost city. The trio appeared to have made no effort to hide their tracks, and did not seem to move with urgency. Quite the opposite.

People who know how a gunshot sounds in a place such as this will understand how startling it is.

How the bird life stops its chatter in an instant, replaced by the fluttering of wings into the air as they take to flight. The echoes are manic, rapid and confusing, hammering off a thousand angled surfaces.

I stopped dead when I heard it, identified the sound as being some distance ahead of me, and began to run, following not just the false echoes, but the spoor they had left behind. I ran so fast that bushes brushed against me as I passed. I tripped once, almost dropping the shotgun, but then I blundered past a maze of pillars that seemed to be the size of small skyscrapers. This was truly like standing in the midst of a city, but with shadows and caverns and caves in the honeycombed rock.

Then I saw the body, lying in the middle of a clear space, still twitching, but clearly dead, with a neat hole through the middle of his forehead. I stepped closer and stared. Terry Yates. The bullet hole was not his only wound: one arm had been mangled in the crash and he was bleeding from his abdomen.

I looked around. The killer was here – there had been no time for him to move far.

Even so, the voice took me by surprise, calling out from some hiding place in the stone.

'He would have slowed us down,' the voice said. 'You can't help people who slow you down. Terry was dying. I just hurried the process.' Hendo's voice echoed from stone to stone and crevice to crevice. It sounded as if it came from above.

I rotated my upper body, trying to ascertain from which direction it had come, impossible here in the clutter of echoes.

I shouted. 'Are you there Malea?'

'Of course she's with me. You can't have her, Mulligan, she's my wife.'

I wasn't sure if then I heard something muffled, as if he had a hand over her mouth and she was trying to speak. 'Where are you?' I called.

'You're a copper, aren't you? Work it out for yourself.'

The echoes made it impossible; hard, cold reflective stone everywhere. I heard sounds of movement, then the voice again.

'I'm going to kill you, Mulligan, you know that, don't you?'

I said nothing.

'And I'll kill her before I let you touch her. I really do love her, you know.'

'But she doesn't love you,' I called back. 'She loves me. You can't steal love from someone. They have to give it to you.' The echoes chattered back and forth from the stone, and for a while there was nothing further.

'I bet you'd love a drink now, wouldn't you, Mulligan? It's been a hard day, imagine how it would feel. Cold beer. It would help, wouldn't it?'

I thought I might have pinpointed the voice. Over towards the sun, a larger pillar with strange hollows, caves, shadows. Maybe ten metres off the ground.

'You'd like to get pissed, Mulligan, wouldn't you? Get drunk like you were that day you killed that girl in your car. What was her name again?'

'Fuck you,' I croaked out.

'I heard she bled a lot. Bled like hell, didn't she?'

The image that came into my mind was one that I did my best to stave off, day after day, night after night.

'Heard that you were half lying on her, bawling your stupid eyes out. You were pissed, weren't you? Pissed out of your stupid head. And you're s'posed to be a cop. S'posed to be locking people up for doing that kind of thing, but you got away with it. They covered it up, didn't they? You walked off scot free. Proud of that, are you, Mulligan?'

I charged towards the place I decided that he was hiding, and only the knowledge that Malea was with him stopped me from firing blindly into every shadow, every nook, sending lead shot deep into his heart, his guts, his brain. I stopped short – a bull goaded beyond all restraint, waiting for the opening of the rodeo gate.

'You want a drink now, don't you, Mulligan, because drink makes you forget, doesn't it? Makes you strong again.'

'No,' I croaked out, 'it makes you weak. Only you don't know it.'

'You're frightened, aren't you, Mulligan? Frightened of finding out that it wasn't the grog that made it happen. You want to blame grog for everything, when all it does is bring out something that's always there in all of us. People like me don't hide it. The rest are just hypocritical ...'

The sound of a chopper came from the distance, thumping across the plains and into the stone valleys and ravines. Moments later the clatter died away as it settled to the earth somewhere. At the road, I guessed, where the Wildcat must be visible from the air for miles.

'It doesn't matter,' Hendo called, 'you're dead inside, Mulligan. You've been like that for a long time, haven't you?'

My voice rose to a scream that rang in the stone, 'Shut up. I'm not.' I turned the barrel of the shotgun skywards and fired, the gun booming in that confined space. I stood, letting the barrel drop, shaking like a leaf.

There was silence while the echoes died, then, 'Why don't you come and find me, Mulligan, I'm not coming out unless you do.'

'You bastard,' I hissed, 'you paid them in grog, and shard. You paid helpless people alcohol and drugs just to make some money.'

'Some money? You're kidding me. Millions. It was brilliant, and worked like a charm until you came along and fucked it up.'

I breathed hard, trying to bring myself under control. He was right. I *had* stopped them. It was over for them. Even if Hendo killed me, I had paid back a little of what I owed to society.

With that realisation I knew I had to get Malea out of danger. I had to make her safe. Hendo was armed, but if he had a rifle he would have picked me off already. It must therefore be a short range weapon, maybe the little automatic I had seen him with, only good for ten or twenty paces. No, he had to draw me close, and use Malea as a shield.

Calm, I told myself. *Look for signs. He came this way, where did he go from here?* I used my eyes like I had been taught. Scanning, looking for anything unusual.

To my left, I saw a spider's web. It was a crucifix spider, not guarding the centre of her web like she normally would, but scuttling away in a corner. One of the four anchor strands had parted, and the spider was in the process of repairing it. As I watched she launched herself from the corner to the nearby stalks of grass, streaming silk all the way. I knew that once she had secured it she would crawl back up to the web, and maybe repeat the journey a few times until all was secure.

Someone had broken that strand, and that meant …

'What are you waiting for, Mulligan? I'm not coming out. If you want the girl you're gonna have to come in here and kill me. Only you won't, 'cause I'll get you first. I was dealing with dogs like you when I was barely outta short pants.'

I stared into the shadows, a hundred shades of grey and black, squinting, trying to find another sign, something beyond that might indicate where they had gone. At first there was nothing, but I made myself concentrate more deeply, the channelling of the senses until they were as sharp as a razor.

Everything changed. I could see the marks on stalks of grass where dew had run down, erasing the dust. The spider web became brilliant silk, catching the sun with a rainbow of highlights. Between the web and the stone faces behind it I saw movement: the blade of a tussock springing up from where it had been flattened some minutes before.

'You still there, Mulligan?' came the voice. I had him worried. Something told me to stay silent.

A minute passed. 'I'm not that stupid. Don't think you'll get me to come out just by shutting up.'

Right now he couldn't see me. Of course, he had watched while I walked into the clearing, but he knew that if he could see me then I could also see him. He was very close. Behind the now straightened grass stalk there was something strange about the stone face. A split perhaps. I didn't know. I stared at the spot, and that was when Ian Henderson made a mistake. Curiosity killed the cat.

Hendo's face appeared from inside the crack just for an instant, then disappeared as fast as it had come. Checking that I was still around. His voice came a moment later.

'Clever boy,' he said. 'You saw me, didn't you?'

I hesitated. 'Yes.'

'Well, what's stopping you?'

Now for the first time he must have taken his hand away from Malea's face. 'Don't, Ben, don't come near us. He's got a gun ...'

The words were cut off abruptly and I started forward, stopping myself from a headlong rush only with difficulty.

'Well now,' Hendo went on, 'how about I break one of these pretty little fingers. So easy to do ...'

Malea's scream made up my mind for me. I loped for the spot, the shotgun held ahead of me like a spear. I came around the rock face, seeing him for the first time. He was holding Malea close like a shield around his body, one arm extended with the ugly little gun pointing at my chest.

The pistol discharged as I went for him and I felt the bullet pass close to my ear. I could not shoot back but lifted the shotgun by the stock and brought it down hard into his face, feeling bone and gristle disintegrate under the blow. The handgun fired again, but I seized the hand and twisted it until he dropped it. There was no sense of revenge in me, no need to hurt for its own sake, but merely to neutralise him, put him out of action so I would never need to worry about him again.

Not daring to slacken my grip, I turned to Malea, who had backed away, staring fearfully. 'There are some cable ties in my pocket, can you get them out?' I asked.

I was conscious of her hands working, and then it was just a matter of bringing his wrists together, holding them and getting her to loop first one black plastic tie, then another around them. I drew them tight myself, and rolled him so I could do the ankles. Once these were tight I came to my feet. There was blood on my hands when I took hers and we stood together, saying nothing, Hendo swearing and spitting blood and teeth into the soil.

I heard shouts, running footsteps. The cops, at last, and I was still alive.

'What will happen to you?' Malea asked.

'I don't know.'

'You understand that I will tell the truth.'

'Yes, I know that.'

'Will the truth help?'

'It always helps. Will you wait for me?'

'Don't ask me now. Nothing is the same. My father is in danger.' There were tears in her eyes. 'I need time. Will you give me that?'

I understood. I held my hands high so there was no misunderstanding as the cops came in. I let the handcuffs click around my own wrists, knowing in my heart that Malea and I were as close to understanding each other as two human beings could be. Still, I almost cried out loud when they took me away from her, unsure if I would ever see her again.

Epilogue

AFTER FIVE DAYS spent sorting the mess out in Katherine I walked free. I still had my job, my freedom, and, to my surprise, the respect of my comrades for what I had done. I even made it to the front page of the Northern Territory News, my ugly mug smiling while I shook hands with the Chief Minister. I was happy with the outcome – a team of health workers on their way down to the Roper to try to undo the damage done – along with an internal police enquiry into the circumstances of Chris's defection to the other side.

I made peace with Dale Cooke, the copper I had threatened with the splinter of glass, and we laughed it off together, shook the memory away like crumbs from a blanket. Malea caught a plane back to the Philippines. She landed in Manila while I sat in the eleventh pew of the Anglican Church in Katherine and paid my respects to Eric, a damn good trainee cop, while his mother and aunties bawled their eyes out up the front.

Malea's statements had cut through the lies and bullshit. She had seen the whole thing. Hendo and Wallaby Yates had both been remanded in custody. The surviving Yates brother was okay; a few pinholes here and there and a chipped shin bone. Apparently the bastard would be fit for trial in a few days, charged with the murder of Eric Swanson along with manufacturing, cultivating and trafficking a prohibited substance.

I followed the nationwide hunt for Chris Reilly with interest. He handed himself into a cop station at Cardwell, Queensland. Apparently, by that stage, his wife had left him, and he was as sorry for himself as a man can get.

With two weeks off work to sort myself out I went back to Camp Leichhardt, getting a lift with the new Gajiyuma cop, a young bloke called Lee Sykes, full of enthusiasm and wanting to change the world. He was going to settle in first, and then his wife and two kids would join him down there.

As we pulled in there was no Mayor Davis to come up and warn us about the dust. He was gone, and there was a warrant out for his arrest. I doubted he would be hard to find. In a way, I felt sorry for him – the poor old bastard just wanted to make an easy quid. Problem is, making money at the expense of the well-being of others just isn't on.

Lee dropped me at my campsite. My boat was on the trailer, and Chook and his missus had folded up my tent, rolled my swag and packed them into the boat with a tarp neatly covering it all.

After Lee waved and disappeared down the track, Chook and Shirl came over. Then, in ones and twos, they all turned up. The Trout. Konrad. Roy and Christo. Col Alexander. These strange old bastards with their little dogs, their stories of love and life – old ladies knitting endless winter scarves, spending their final years doing what they love, in this paradise that we are so damn lucky to have.

I looked around at the Grey Nomads. As Chook said, the old girls might not look good naked anymore, but of course they felt good when it was dark and cold and you needed someone to cuddle up to. The same, I'm sure, could be said about the men. These funny, interesting couples loved each other. Love is in the skin and the nerve endings as well as the heart. They were bringing their love from Ballarat and Deniliquin; Cowra, Toowoomba and Keith; bringing it here into paradise for a few years before they slip away from this earth and their relatives gather in churches all over the country to say goodbye, to farewell them into whatever it is that follows life.

One of my great pleasures that day was to present Maggie the biologist with the most expensive genuine thermos I could find in Katherine. It cost a bomb, but was an absolute beauty – powder coated stainless steel and guaranteed for life. After I had handed it over she gave me a little peck on the cheek and there was something wistful in her eyes, 'You know,' she said, 'if I was just a few years younger ...'

I was pleased things were the way they were, because I had already given my heart away. It wouldn't do to complicate things.

Chook gave me a hand with the Toyota – I'd brought out a set of leads to replace those cut by the Yates boys. It took an hour, and she needed a jump start to get going, but once she warmed up the engine chattered away like good diesels do.

When it was done we went back to Chook's camp for a feed, and he hesitated at the icebox. 'You want a beer, or what?'

I grinned back at him, and shook my head. Then for some reason the question struck me as funny, and I laughed fit to bust.

Before dawn the following day, I was out on the river. I would have tried the lagoon but I didn't have the emotional strength to go there alone. Without her.

Instead I fished a creek mouth four miles downstream from Camp Leichhardt, and there I pulled from the water four glittering barramundi. The fish were beauties. Ancient, glowing silver, and captured in a fair contest. One on one. I let two of them go and kept two for the table.

At the end of the day I made the Stessl fast and backed the trailer down, winching her on while I listened to a pair of orange-collared lorikeets squabble in a tree branch, and the ramp croc eyed me from his haunt under the overhanging mangroves, waiting for his dinner. When I had filleted the fish and chucked the frames out, I drove back to camp.

The fire that I had left to die down had flames leaping high from a bundle of fresh fuel. A familiar female figure looked up from the camp table where she was chopping onions. I parked the Toyota, got out and stared.

Malea turned. 'Did you get any fish?'

'Yeah, four, and I brought two home.'

'Good, there isn't much food in the Engel. We might need to run into Roper Bar for bread tomorrow.'

'How did you get back here?'

'I got a lift with a lovely young woman and her children. She's coming out to join her husband at the ...'

For a moment, with my arms around her, Malea tried valiantly to continue chopping onions. Then, giving up, she put down the knife and turned inside the circle of my arms. The kiss she planted on my lips was soft and welcoming.

'I can hardly believe this is happening,' I said.

She shook her head, tears so thick they made a lens in the corner of each eye.

'I am here,' she said, 'with you. Nothing else matters. Not anymore.'

Crime, history, and international politics are all passionate interests of author Greg Barron. He has lived in North America, New South Wales and in and around Katherine, Northern Territory. He once crossed Arnhem Land on foot and has a passion for outback landscapes.

Published by HarperCollins Australia and Stories of Oz Publishing, Greg's books are gutsy page-turners that have won a wide readership and critical acclaim.

Gjbarron@outlook.com
Facebook.com/storiesofoz
Facebook.com/gregbarronauthor
gregbarron.com.au

ALL BOOKS AVAILABLE AT OZBOOKSTORE.COM